Camden Town Tales

Camden Town Tales

The
Celeb
Next
Door

Hilary Freeman

Piccadilly Press • London

To my parents,
Michael and Vivien Freeman

First published in Great Britain in 2011
by Piccadilly Press Ltd,
5 Castle Road, London NW1 8PR
www.piccadillypress.co.uk

A catalogue record for this book is available
from the British Library

ISBN: 978 1 84812 084 6 (paperback)

1 3 5 7 9 10 8 6 4 2

Printed in the UK by CPI Bookmarque Ltd,
Croydon, CR1 4PD
Cover design by Simon Davis
Cover illustrations by Susan Hellard

Hi!

I grew up in boring suburbia so, by the time I was a teenager, I longed for excitement, noise and colour. I found it in Camden Town. On Sundays, my friends and I would travel to Camden Market to buy vintage jeans, get henna tattoos and exchange friendship bracelets. Later, we started going to gigs in Camden and to the Camden Palace nightclub (now KOKO).

As soon as I got my first job in London, I knew exactly where I wanted to live – it had to be Camden. I rented a flat on the high street and fell in love with the area all over again – and I'm still here. You can be whoever you want to be in Camden – trendy, quirky, straight, or even a bit mad – nobody minds.

Camden Town Tales is about a group of friends who all live on the same fictional street in Camden. There's celebrity-obsessed Rosie, who's not quite as sophisticated as she thinks; Vix, her more thoughtful best friend; and Sky, whose mum is an embarrassing hippy. Together, they hang out at the market, go to gigs, spot celebrities, fall in love and sometimes fall out with each other.

I hope the books will make you love Camden as much as I do!

Love,

Hilary

Prologue

I can't believe I'm here. In the VIP tent. On the friends and family guest list!

Regent's Park has been transformed for the festival. There are two huge stages at either end of the green space, and stalls everywhere selling food, clothes and band merchandise. There are thousands of people here and the atmosphere is amazing. It's like a giant, outdoor, all-day party.

Max and I are just walking out of the tent to have a wander when I spot a familiar face. It's Lisa, a girl from my year, and two of her equally bitchy mates, and they're hanging around by the entrance, waiting to see who comes out. Lisa is not, and never has been, my friend. Until now, it seems.

'Rosie!' she screams in excitement. 'Oh my God, it's good to see you! What are you doing here?' She rushes over to my side, leaving her friends to trot after her. 'Hey, did I see you just come out of the VIP tent? How come?'

'Hey, Lisa.' I beam at her and let her kiss me on the cheek. 'I'm here because I know the guys in the band.' I fiddle with my red wristband and try not to look too smug. 'Rufus Justice is my next-door neighbour. And,' I nod towards Max, who is right next to me, holding my hand, 'this is my boyfriend Max – Rufus's brother.'

Lisa gives me exactly the reaction I am hoping for. Her eyes grow round and huge and, even though she's at least three inches taller than me, I could swear that she's looking up at me in awe. It's a shame it's the summer holidays. Lisa has such a big mouth that if it were term-time, the news of my celebrity romance would have spread round the school within a day.

'Oh right, cool,' she says, and I can tell she's itching to ask if I can get her a VIP pass too, but she doesn't have the guts to ask.

As amazing as it feels, I have to check myself. How did I, Rosie Buttery, suddenly become someone worth knowing?

I guess it all began one Sunday afternoon, a few weeks before the summer holidays . . .

2

Chapter 1

The Celebometer

'**G**uess what, Vix!' My voice must be louder than I think because the people walking past me turn around to stare. 'I have just spotted *the* most amazing celebrity in Costa Coffee. I had to go in to make sure. I swear it was him!'

I wait for Vix to ask me who, but she doesn't, so I tell her anyway. 'It was Adam Grigson, the guy from the vampire film. He smiled at me too.' OK, he was probably aiming it at the woman standing behind me, but that's just a technicality: he did smile in my general direction.

'Cool, well done, Rosie,' replies Vix, not very enthusiastically.

3

Now I can't help wishing I'd phoned Sky first instead.

'You've got to admit that it's a pretty amazing spot, Vix. A fifty-pointer. And it puts me way in the lead.'

'Sure,' Vix agrees. 'By the way, I forgot to mention that I spotted someone too. Earlier.'

'Yeah? So why didn't you call? Tell me . . . Go on . . .'

'Didn't seem that important. And I can't remember her name . . .'

'Young? Old? Fat? I need a bit more to go on.'

'Oh you know, thingy . . .' Vix sounds frustrated. 'From that soap you like. The one with the big hair.'

'Oh, *thingy*. Yeah, right. You mean Cheryl-Anne Taylor. You can't have full points if you don't know her name. I'll give you . . . seven.'

'Fine,' says Vix. She laughs. 'Whatever. You take it so seriously, Rosie, anyone would think you were competing in the Olympics, or something.'

Maybe I do take the game a bit too seriously, but I want my friends to play it properly. It's called the Celebometer and I made it up on my way back from Camden Market one Sunday afternoon a few weeks ago. There are always so many actors and musicians and TV presenters in Camden Town that it seems a shame not to turn spotting them into a sport.

The rules are simple: if you spot somebody you recognise, you have to call or text at least one of your friends to record it. Points are awarded according to the spotee's level of fame, how fanciable they are and whether you manage to make eye contact or talk to them. I haven't decided what the prize is. I think I'll just make it up as I go along. I'm good at that.

But if Vix doesn't feel like joining in today, I'm not going to force her.

'Look, Vix, it's fine by me if you don't want to play, really.'

She sighs. 'It's not that. It was fun to start with. It just feels like all you ever want to talk about these days is which celebrity you've seen. I'd rather talk about real stuff sometimes, you know?'

'Sure. Course.' I didn't realise I was doing that. 'I'm sorry.'

'Don't worry about it, hun,' she says, affectionately.

'So are you coming round tonight?'

'I can't, I'm sorry. Mum wants the whole family to have dinner together. I've got no choice, worse luck.'

'Poor you. I guess I'll see you tomorrow, then, on the way to school. And we'll chat online later, of course. I'll go and see what Sky is up to. I'm just turning into our street now. Bye, then . . .'

I have lived in Paradise Avenue, a hotch-potch of a street in Camden Town, all my life. My best friends Sky and Vix live here too. It isn't a particularly long street, but it is a strange-looking one. None of the buildings match. At one end of the street there's a council block and, at the other, several big Victorian houses. I live in one of these — number seventeen — not because I'm rich, but because it's been in my family for about sixty years.

Visitors always comment that Paradise Avenue has 'character' — and so do the people who live on it. As well as lawyers and business people and doctors, like my mum who works at the local health centre, there are some eccentric old ladies living in the sheltered housing block, and several writers and musicians. If you walk down the street at night, you are bound to hear a band practising, a guitar teacher giving lessons, or an opera singer rehearsing her scales.

There are also some people on Paradise Avenue whom you might want to avoid. There's a very weird man who never cuts or washes his hair and spends all day in the betting shop, and a group of squatters who have taken over an empty house and turned it into an 'art collective'.

Paradise Avenue certainly isn't a street to live on if you like peace and quiet. But nobody chooses to live in Camden Town for that.

I'm at Sky's flat now. I ring her doorbell, hoping that she'll answer, and not her mother. It's not that I don't like Sky's mum, I'm just not in the mood for chatting to her today. She's one of those mums who insists on you calling her by her first name (Rebecca) and asking you about what you've been up to, as if she's your friend too. Sky says it's because she's lonely since her dad left, but it can be really embarrassing, especially when she tries to act like a teenager and wants to talk about boys or come out to the market with us.

It makes me glad that my mum is straight-laced and boring, like mums should be. I'm also very grateful that my parents gave me and my brother Charlie normal names. Sky's sisters are called Ocean and Grass. That would be fine if they all lived on a hippie commune somewhere in India, but not when they have to go to the local comprehensive in the middle of London. Especially when their surname is Smith.

'Hello?' Sky's voice blares through the intercom, making me jump.

'Hey, it's me. Can I come up?'

'Yes! Thank God it's you. Mum's expecting some of her weird friends for dinner. Come up, please.'

She's at the top of the stairs, waiting to greet me, when I arrive. She looks far too groomed for a Sunday evening at home, with her glossy, dark hair styled perfectly, and a stretchy black dress. Sky doesn't do casual. 'Save me,' she mouths, as we hug.

I giggle and try not to notice the weird smell coming from the kitchen. 'You can come round to mine if you like.'

'Unfortunately, I can't. Mum wants me to accompany her on the guitar. They're singing sixteenth-century madrigals. Don't you dare say anything . . .'

'I wouldn't dream of it,' I say, but I can't help smirking. 'Maybe you could add a bit of rapping in the middle.'

Sky motions as if to slap me. I duck. 'So what have you been up to since I saw you earlier?'

'Just hanging out at the shops. Hey, I almost forgot to tell you: I had the most amazing star spot before . . .'

Sky is far more impressed than Vix at the mention of Adam Grigson's name. 'Seriously? Like, wow!' she says. She is as celebrity mad as me, if not more, mainly because it annoys her mum, who thinks celebrity culture is the worst thing ever to happen to society and will lead to the end of the world. 'You should have spoken to him. I wonder what he was doing in Camden.'

'I heard there's a film being made around here. I saw some location vans the other day. Oh my God, do you think they might have been filming in the cafe? Maybe I'll be in it, in the background, like an extra.'

'They wouldn't have you,' says Sky, grinning. 'You'd keep waving at the cameras, just to make sure you were seen.'

'That's not fair.' I pout, comically (my 'trout pout' look, Sky calls it). 'Although you're probably right.'

We go into Sky's bedroom, put on some music and sit on her bed and chat for a while. From outside in the hall we hear the intercom buzz several times, and then the chatter of high-pitched voices. There's a knock on the door and before Sky can say anything, her mum pushes it open. She's wearing a long, loose, linen dress, and – very obviously – no bra. I try not to look.

'Hello, Rosie,' she says, smiling at me. 'Why didn't you come to say hello? It would have been lovely to talk to you.'

'Sorry, Mrs . . . Rebecca,' I tell her, sheepishly.

Sky nudges me in the ribs with her elbow, which makes me want to laugh.

'Now, would you like to stay for dinner? Do you sing or play an instrument? We're having a music night.'

'I'm tone deaf, Rebecca.' That's a lie, but I'm sure it's only a little white one. 'I'd ruin it.' Which is definitely the truth.

'Oh no, I'm certain you wouldn't. You could play the tambourine.'

Sky nudges me again and this time I have to try really hard to suppress a giggle. I hold my breath but it bursts out of me, like a snort. 'Thanks so much, Rebecca, but honestly, I don't want to spoil your evening. Anyway, I said I'd be home for dinner.'

'That's OK.' She smiles. 'In that case, Rosie, I don't mean to be rude, but would you mind making your way home soon? We need to make a start.'

'Not at all, er, Rebecca.' I clamber up from the bed. 'I'll go now.' I kiss Sky and make the shape of a phone with my hand. 'Laters.'

Sky catches my eye and nods furiously. 'Save me,' she mouths again, and I purse my lips in sympathy.

It's almost dusk now and there aren't many people about, just a couple strolling to the nearby pub. I don't recognise them, but strangers often use my street as a short cut to the main road. My house is at the far end, a few minutes' walk from Sky's flat.

As I walk, I wonder if there's anything good on television tonight. I've got that empty Sunday evening feeling, the dread of having to get up early tomorrow and face a whole week at school. Next weekend is such a long way away.

I'm so engrossed in my thoughts that, as I approach my house, I almost don't notice the large removal lorry parked outside the house next door.

'Careful, love,' says a man, carrying a large box. He narrowly avoids bumping into me. 'This stuff is expensive.'

'Oh God, sorry.' I stop and look around me. Now I can see that there are other men carrying boxes from the lorry into the house. It's the largest house on the street and it's been empty for almost a year. There's been lots of building work going on at the house for the past few months – annoying drilling and knocking sounds, which have driven me mad. It's hard enough to do my homework when there aren't any distractions.

Now somebody is finally moving in. Will there be a girl my age, or even better, a fit boy? Knowing my luck, it will be a family with young kids, or some old people who'll ask me to turn my music down when it isn't even loud.

'Is someone moving in?' I ask one of the removal men. It's a stupid question and I know it. I'm just not sure how else to broach the subject. 'I live next door, you see.'

'Yeah,' says the man. 'Young guy. Think he's some sort of musician.' He gestures to the house and then points to the large, antique wooden table he's off-loading from the lorry. 'Must be doing all right for himself, eh?'

I nod. A musician sounds promising, especially a rich, successful one. 'Do you mind if I stand here a while?'

'Feel free,' says the removal man, who is out of breath and sweaty. 'No skin off my nose.'

I lean up against the wall and look at the objects being unloaded from the lorry. As well as furniture and boxes of CDs, there is what looks like expensive studio recording equipment.

I'm beginning to feel a bit cold now and thinking I should go inside because Mum will be wondering where I am, when I hear a clattering from the lorry and a 'Whoops, careful!' followed by something much ruder from one of the removal men. Three of them are struggling with something they've clearly been told to treat with care.

Curious, I walk closer. It's a huge drum kit. So, my new neighbour is a drummer? Drummers aren't quite as cool as guitarists or singers, but at least they won't complain about the noise from next door.

And then I notice something that makes me look again

in disbelief: the word *Fieldstar* and a squiggly star logo emblazoned on the front of the drum kit in bright red, luminous paint. I've seen this kit before, so many times, on TV and in pictures in magazines (and in posters on my walls). That logo means that the kit can only belong to one person: Rufus Justice, the drummer for my favourite band, Fieldstar.

My hand is already twitching for my phone. I can't wait to tell Vix and Sky the most thrilling news they'll have heard all year. The gorgeous and talented Rufus Justice is going to be my next-door neighbour!

Surely that must be worth at least five thousand points on the Celebometer scale. In fact, there is no competition. Game over!

Chapter 2

Meet The Butterys

Nobody takes much notice of me when I come in, but I'm used to that. Dad is in his 'studio' (the spare room), finishing his latest abstract masterpiece, Charlie is in his bedroom playing on his computer, and Mum is preparing dinner.

'Mum, you'll never believe it, but Rufus Justice is moving in next door!' I announce as I walk into the kitchen. 'Isn't that amazing?'

'Who?' says Mum, distracted.

'Rufus Justice! From Fieldstar!'

'Oh,' says Mum. 'Am I supposed to have heard of him?'

'Derr, yes. I've only got every album Fieldstar ever made

and posters of them all over my bedroom wall. And you bought me tickets to their gig for my birthday, remember?'

'Oh, right. And which one is Rufus?'

'The gorgeous one – well, they're all gorgeous. The one with the big pecs and the sticky-out hair. The drummer.'

Mum looks concerned. 'He's far too old for you,' she says, stirring furiously.

'He's only twenty-one. Anyway, he's moving in next door, I'm not planning to date him.' Although, come to think of it, that is a fantastic possibility. 'Hey, I wonder if he's going to register at your surgery. Then you'll know everything about him.'

'You know I can't reveal information like that. It's confidential,' says Mum, in her serious doctor's voice.

'Yeah, I know. Boring.' I didn't really expect her to help. I shrug and start to walk out of the kitchen.

'Don't forget dinner's nearly ready,' Mum calls after me. 'Five minutes, OK?'

'OK.' I make my way upstairs. I'm hoping that Dad might be a little more interested in my exciting news. He really likes one of Fieldstar's tracks, the anthemic one that everyone sings along with at festivals. He says it helps him to concentrate when he's painting. Walls, that is, not masterpieces. Dad is an artist, but he's only ever sold one painting, so he makes his living as a decorator. Painting canvasses is what he does in his spare time.

'Hey, Dad.' I open the studio door. He is covered in

paint. It's on his glasses, his cheeks, even in his hair, disguising his bald spot quite efficiently.

'Rosie, come and have a look,' he says. He steps back from his easel and studies the thick splotches of red and blue paint on his canvas. 'What do you think? I've done a lot to it since you last saw it.'

'Nice,' I tell him. I can't see any difference at all, but I don't want to hurt his feelings. 'What are you calling it, again?'

'*The Quiet Death of the Tarantula*,' he says. There is pride in his voice.

'You should sell your paintings at Camden Market,' I suggest. 'I know someone who could get you a pitch.'

Dad sighs. 'Oh no, I'm a serious artist.'

'I know, Dad.' I smile at him. Poor Dad, I wish he could get a break.

'I've got something to tell you . . .' I begin, hopefully. 'Rufus Justice from Fieldstar is moving into the Robsons' old place. Isn't that cool?'

'You're kidding me,' says Dad. 'Who told you that?'

'I saw some removal men unloading his stuff. There's recording equipment and everything. I wonder if the rest of the band will come round. And then maybe we can jam.'

I really should practise my guitar more often . . . I've only mastered two chords so far, but it hurts my fingers so much.

Dad starts to whistle his favourite Fieldstar track and sways his hips in time to the rhythm. It's a little embarrassing when he does that.

'All right, Dad,' I say, and I head for the door. 'Mum says dinner will be ready in a few minutes.' Which just about gives me time to text Vix and Sky with the amazing news.

Dinner is as chaotic as usual. Dad is in a world of his own, probably contemplating red and blue tarantulas dying quietly, and Mum has to keep answering the phone because she's on call tonight. My phone keeps beeping too with texts from Sky and Vix who want all the details, and my little brother Charlie won't sit still. In my opinion, there's only one point to having a brother: if he's older than you and can introduce you to his friends. A little brother, particularly one who is seven years younger, is useless. All Charlie does is leave his toys everywhere, make a racket and chase after you, pretending to shoot you with whatever object he can find. Charlie is officially a pain. I would much prefer to have a sister, even one far younger. At least I could teach her about clothes and make-up and plait her hair.

After dinner, Charlie scuttles off to his bedroom and returns with his football. He hands it to me, with a pleading look, like a pet dog that wants you to play fetch. 'Will you play footie with me, Rosie?' he asks. He's oblivious to my indifference towards him, which is quite sweet. 'You can be goalie and I'll be the striker.'

'Oh Charlie, I've got stuff to do,' I say, groaning. 'Can't you play on your own?'

Charlie looks crestfallen.

'Play with your brother for ten minutes,' says Mum, who clearly just wants him out of her hair.

'OK, OK.' It's not like I have anything else to do.

We go out into the back garden and I lean against the wall, while Charlie tries to aim the ball in my direction. I decide to let him score. He runs towards me cheering and throws his arms around my middle, giving me a big, awkward hug.

'Wuh-un-nil, wuh-un-nil, wuh-un-nil,' he sings. 'It's your turn, Rosie. You can be Wayne Rooney.'

Reluctantly, I walk forward and let Charlie stand in front of the wall in my place. I place the ball at my feet and take a step backwards, ready to take aim. I've already decided I'm going to miss the goal and let Charlie win, when I remember that if I stand on tiptoe I can just see over the wall into the house next door. Rufus Justice's house. There's a glass patio and, when the lights are on, you can get a pretty good view inside the house. Of course, there aren't any lights on at the moment; nobody's living there yet. But soon . . . I wonder if Rufus will have parties in the house, with celebrity guests. Over the summer he might have barbecues in the garden, and I'll be able to talk to him over the wall . . .

'Come on, Rosie,' says Charlie, propelling me out of my fantasy. 'Aim!'

I run forward and, as Charlie dives to the left, I deliberately miss-kick the ball into a flower bed. He giggles and picks himself up from the ground. He's covered in dirt. 'Girls are rubbish at football,' he says, triumphantly. 'I win.'

'Yes, you do,' I agree. 'Well done you.'

Later, alone in my bedroom, I prepare for the week ahead. I put my schoolbooks in my bag and pick out the clothes I'll wear tomorrow. Vix and I go to the same school, the girls' school which is about ten minutes' walk up the road. It's a comprehensive, and you don't have to wear a uniform, but it's really hard to get into and lots of famous people went there in the past. Sky attends the mixed comprehensive nearby, partly because that's where her older sisters go, and partly because her mum didn't manage to do the paperwork for the girls' school in time. I wish all three of us were at the same school, so we could walk in together and gossip about the same people. Sometimes Sky says she feels left out. Then again, the good thing about Sky's school is that she has guy friends she can introduce us all to. There are only boys in the sixth form at my school, and they'll only talk to the sixth form girls.

I hate Sunday evening, because I know I'll have to get up early tomorrow, and then there are five more sleeps until the weekend. But maybe this week will be less boring than usual; maybe I'll be making a new celebrity friend. Before I go to bed I text Vix and Sky goodnight and I plug in my MP3 player, so I can listen to Fieldstar's latest album until I fall asleep. As my eyes begin to close, I wonder if Rufus Justice will soon be sleeping on the other side of the wall.

Chapter 3
A Celebrity Moves In

Rufus Justice moves in to his new house on Tuesday morning, while I'm at school.

At four o'clock, the second the final bell rings, Vix and I escape together and, as we always do on a Tuesday, meet Sky in the café up the road. Over milky hot chocolate and a blueberry muffin divided into three uneven chunks, we discuss the day in forensic detail. Anything to delay going home to homework and our families. None of us is in a good mood: Vix and I had a maths test, which didn't go very well, and Sky had a row with her boyfriend, Rich.

'I can't believe Rich blanked you like that,' I tell Sky,

when she's filled us in on the argument.

'It's so out of order,' says Vix, who has never had a proper boyfriend herself. Plenty of boys like her – she's got that blond, rosy-cheeked, girl-next-door thing going on – but she always turns them down. She's too choosy, or too scared, or both – I'm not sure which. I've tried to talk to her about it but she gets embarrassed.

'Yeah,' I add. 'I hope you showed him he can't diss you like that.'

'I was really offish,' Sky insists. She is obviously more in love with Rich than she wants anyone to know. 'But he's going to call me later so we can have a proper talk. By the way . . .' she says, changing the subject, because she doesn't like it when we criticise Rich. 'I've been meaning to say, I love your new top, Rosie. It suits you.'

'Thanks, Sky.' I smile. I am wearing a stripy top today – not in tribute to Rufus Justice, who only ever wears stripy tops, in various colour combinations – but because the naval look is in and I bought it at the weekend from a Camden Market army and navy surplus stall. It's a little bit big for me, and a little bit long, because it was designed for a Russian sailor with broad shoulders and a slim torso, not for an English girl who is petite and slightly pear-shaped. It only cost eight pounds though, and it's authentic, unlike the copies you'll find in the high street chain stores.

I buy most of my clothes from the market; it makes my

allowance go a lot further, and I'm far more likely to find something original, like a Fifties prom dress or even a Victorian lace bolero. The majority of my friends feel the same way and so we all go clothes hunting together most weekends. Only Sky, who has spent her life in tie-dyed cotton hand-me-downs and thrift-shop finds, refuses to buy market clothes. She likes whatever she can find in TopShop and Miss Selfridge, particularly if it's short and tight and made out of polyester. It's the same with her hair. As soon as she could afford to, she rebelled by having her waist-length dark waves cut into a glossy bob with a fringe. Her mum cried.

The café owner is giving us dirty looks, so we decide it's time to leave. We have been sitting over a plate of crumbs for half an hour because we can't afford to order anything else.

'Oh my God!' Sky almost yells, as we turn into Paradise Avenue. 'Look, the lights are on in Rufus's house. He must have moved in.'

'Seriously?' I say, peering past her to see for myself. I'm so excited I think I might burst. 'Oh my gosh, I think you're right. Come on, let's go and have a peek.'

The three of us scope out Rufus's house, trying as hard as we can to see through the blackout blinds or shutters he's had installed at every window.

'There's no way to see in – it's like a fortress,' says Sky. 'It's so annoying.'

'We could ring the doorbell and just say hello,' says Vix. 'What's the harm?'

Sky giggles. 'Go on then, Vix, you first.'

'No, you go first. You want to meet him much more than me. He's only a person.'

One behind the other, we walk right up to the front door and Sky tentatively sticks out her index finger. It hovers above the doorbell. 'I can't,' she says, stepping away. 'I'm too nervous. Rosie?'

'OK . . .' I lift up my arm to try, then immediately snatch it back. I have the most enormous butterflies flapping about in my belly. They might even be birds. 'No, I can't, I'm not ready. I need to think about what I'm going to say.'

'Wuss,' says Vix. She turns away. 'I'm bored now. I'm going to leave you to it. Speak later, OK?' She gives us each a peck on the cheek and walks slowly back to her house. Just before she goes inside she gives us a little wave.

'Is she all right?' I ask Sky. 'She's been a bit offish lately.'

'Has she? I haven't noticed.'

'Really? Oh, maybe it's just me, then. Which is worse. I get the feeling she's annoyed with me, but I don't know why.' Vix is my oldest friend, and I can sense when something's not right. It's been bothering me for a few days. 'She doesn't even seem that interested in Rufus moving in.'

'Don't worry about it,' Sky reassures me. 'I think she's

just a bit over the whole celebrity thing and . . . Just have a chat with her, yeah?'

'Mmm,' I say. 'I'll try.'

'So are we going to do this, then?' she asks. We're still hovering outside Rufus's front door. 'We could just ring the bell and run away. Maybe he'll come out and then we can pretend we were just walking past, and blame some kids.'

'Too risky. He might spot us. For all we know he's watching us right now. You know, he probably has a security camera. Or one of those two-way mirrors.' Oh God, I think, he could do. He might be looking me straight in the eye at this very moment, and I don't know it. The idea makes me double over with laughter. 'Oh God, how embarrassing. Do you think it's true?'

'Hope not! Can you imagine? Listen, Rosie, I think I'm going to go home too. Neither of us has got the guts to do this now, and I want to make sure I'm in to speak to Rich. Why don't we try again tomorrow?'

'Sure,' I say. But I don't like giving up. 'I'm going to go home too and come up with a plan. In fact, I already have an idea . . .'

I let myself into my house and head straight for the kitchen. I have remembered that in TV shows people always take casseroles or muffins to their new neighbours, as a welcoming gift. I imagine myself arriving at Rufus's door with a wicker basket filled with just-baked goodies, covered by a navy and white gingham cloth. 'A gift, to welcome you to the street,' I'll say, with a perfect smile (in my fantasy, I don't have braces) and he will then, of course, invite me in for a friendly chat . . .

But when I look in the cupboards and in the fridge, all I can find is a packet of Jaffa Cakes, a few blackening bananas, and some leftover couscous. 'Squishy banana, Rufus?' It probably won't do. I need a plan B.

That plan B comes in the unexpected form of Charlie.

'Hello, Rosie,' he says, padding into the kitchen, clutching his ball. 'Wanna play footie again with me?'

Now usually, I would say, 'No way, Squirt, not today,' especially as Mum isn't home yet to harangue me and Dad's out of earshot upstairs. But I've had a brainwave. Playing football with Charlie could just be my way into Rufus's house.

'OK, Charlie,' I say, with a mischievous smile. 'That would be fun.'

We wander into the garden and I head straight for the wall. 'I'll be goalie first, OK?'

I let Charlie score a couple of times, before putting my cunning plan into action. 'Let's try something new, OK?' I suggest. 'I know you can kick the ball harder than you do. You're really strong, aren't you?'

Charlie beams. 'Yes, course I am,' he says. He runs at the ball as fast as his little legs will carry him, and kicks it up into the air with an excited yelp. It strikes the wall just to the left of my head. I retrieve it and hand it back to him.

'Well done! Now, go on, Charlie, do it again. But kick the ball really hard, as high as you can. Yes, take a run up to it and whack it really hard . . . That's it . . . Again . . . Go on! See how far you can make it fly.'

This time the ball bounces higher, hitting the top of the wall. My eyes follow it, as it appears to hesitate in mid-air, before falling gently to the other side. Yes! Secretly, I clench my fist in victory.

'Oh, Charlie,' I scold. 'You've kicked it into next door's garden. Now I'm going to have to go next door and fetch it. You silly boy.'

Charlie pouts. 'Sorry Rosie,' he says. 'I didn't mean to. Don't tell Mum.'

'Course I won't.' Charlie looks so bereft that I feel a tiny bit guilty, but it's more than worth it. 'Stay here and I'll go and get it. OK?'

He nods and I pat him on the head, affectionately.

Maybe little brothers aren't quite so pointless, after all.

Chapter 4

The Rufus Justice

efore I go round to Rufus's house, I put on lip gloss and smooth down my hair frizz with serum. If I'm honest, I wouldn't usually do this before going round to retrieve a football from a neighbour's garden, but Rufus is not a regular neighbour, is he? He's a celebrity neighbour and, therefore, worthy of a little effort.

I stand on his doorstep breathing fast for a few minutes before daring to ring the doorbell. My heart is pounding and I can feel that my face is flushed. Oh my God, oh my God, I think, it's finally going to happen; I'm finally going to meet him. I've rehearsed my speech loads of times in my head. When Rufus opens the door, I'll pretend not to recognise him at first. I'll act like he looks familiar and then slowly pretend I've figured out who he is. 'You're not Rufus Justice, are you?' I'll say, feigning surprise that he's moved in next door. I'll flatter him a bit and then I'll say sorry about my stupid little brother and ask for the ball back. Hopefully, he'll invite me in . . .

The door opens, just a crack. It makes me jump, even though I've been expecting it.

'Ello?' It's a tall, blond, impossibly beautiful woman, with an accent I can't place.

'Oh, hello,' I say, flustered. Who is this woman? I didn't know Rufus had a girlfriend. There goes my rehearsed speech. 'I'm, erm, really sorry,' I stutter. 'I, er, live next door, and I've just kicked my football over your wall. I mean, my brother has. Can I come in and get it? From your garden, I mean? The back one, obviously.'

The woman looks me up and down (more down than up, really, since I only come up to her chest). It's quite intimidating. She nods — she must have decided I seem harmless enough — and opens the door wider. 'Come een,' she says. She has the type of voice that vibrates like a purr. 'You say you leeve nexta door? I'm Isabella.'

'Oh, and I'm Rosie,' I say, trying to stand on tiptoes, which is tricky in my wedge sandals. 'So, er, do you live here alone?'

'No, I leeve here wiz my boyfriend.' Isabella gives me a knowing look, which says, 'Who are you trying to kid?

You and I both know who my boyfriend is.'

I blush. I hope she doesn't think I'm just another groupie, desperate for a glimpse of Rufus. She sighs loudly and leads me into the hall. Through the open door of the living room I catch a glimpse of him and my butterflies flap wildly in my tummy. 'Oh!' I say, pretending to be surprised. 'Is *that* your boyfriend?' My voice is all squeaky with excitement.

Isabella nods. 'Yes,' she says. 'Vould you like to meet heem?'

'Could I? I mean, if it's all right? I mean, yes please.'

Isabella nods again. She shows me into the living room and leaves me there, before disappearing upstairs. Rufus doesn't look up. He's sitting on the edge of an enormous cream sofa, holding a Wii Nunchuk and staring hard at a huge plasma TV. He's gorgeous, I think, although maybe not quite as gorgeous as he is in the poster on my bedroom wall. On my wall he's had a shave. And he isn't wearing brown socks with holes in.

I wait a moment for him to notice me but he doesn't budge. Bravely, I walk right up to him. 'I'm Rosie Buttery, your new next-door neighbour,' I say. My legs are shaky and I hope he can't tell. God knows why, but I've got a stupid urge to hum one of Fieldstar's songs, which is playing over and over in my head.

'Hi, Rosie, nice to meet you,' says Rufus, who can't ignore me now that I'm standing right in front of him. He puts down his Nunchuk and holds out his hand, palm upwards. He doesn't introduce himself; it's clear he assumes that everyone he meets already knows his name.

I'm not sure if he wants to shake my hand or give me a high-five, so we end up doing this embarrassing kind of half clap, half holding hands thing. I blush even more. But it doesn't seem to bother Rufus.

'Um, er, so how are you?' I ask. 'Oh yeah, and welcome to our street.'

'Thanks,' says Rufus, grinning. He doesn't ask me anything, so I stand there like an idiot, waiting. I've always wondered if Rufus Justice is a stage name. Now, it's the only thing I can think about – the rest of my brain is a giant void. 'So is Rufus Justice your real name?' I blurt out.

He smirks. 'Yes, it's one hundred per cent real. My parents are Mr and Mrs Justice. I was christened Rufus.' He stares at me intensely. 'Is Buttery your real name? Buttery! Surely not.'

I turn even redder, if that's possible. 'Yeah, honestly. It's a super-old English name from, like, when the Normans invaded in 1066. I googled it once. My family fought at the Battle of Hastings and everything.'

'Oh, cool,' says Rufus. His eyes twinkle and he grins naughtily, as if he's just had the most incredible, original thought. 'Hey,' he says, pointing at me, 'I can't believe it's not buttery!' He laughs at his own joke.

I'm not laughing. If your name is Buttery, you hear this

type of thing all the time. But, as it's *the* Rufus Justice, I smile and say, 'Funny. Clever. Very good.'

'Lucky your parents didn't call you Marge . . . Hey, now I'm – no *you're* – on a roll!'

I've heard both of these before too. A million times. I force a smile. Dad always tells me that if you can't beat them, you should join them. So I say, 'Now, you're spreading the joke a little thin,' and giggle.

He doesn't get it, or maybe he just isn't listening. 'Well, I'd better get going Ms Buttery,' he says. 'Things to do.' He points in the direction of his Wii console.

'Oh right, yes, sure.' Is that it? I want to say, 'Can I have your number?' or, 'Maybe we could hang out,' like I would to any normal new friend or neighbour, but he's a rock star, and it doesn't seem appropriate. Instead I say, 'Right, see you around,' and, when he doesn't move, I head into the hall to see myself out.

The walls are still the same muddy colour that the Robsons painted them. Not a rock star's style at all, I think. I'm already opening the front door when I have an idea. It's a quite brilliant idea. Steeling myself, I turn around and walk straight back into the room I've just left. 'Er, sorry to bother you,' I mumble. Rufus is engrossed in his game, manically banging away on his games console. It's a drumming game, and it's very noisy. 'Er, ahem,' I say again, a little louder. I clear my throat. 'Excuse me.'

Rufus taps out a little drum roll, just like he does on

stage, and turns to face me. 'Yes?' he says. He looks mildly annoyed. 'I was just winning there, although,' he boasts, 'I should do, given that I helped design the game.'

'Wow!' I splutter, remembering just how famous he is. He's only the best drummer in the country. 'Um, I'm sorry to bother you again. It's just that I couldn't help noticing your walls . . . In case you wanted them painting. My dad's a painter and decorator, you see, and he could give you a really good price, and he's just next door . . .'

'Yeah?' says Rufus. 'I have already got some quotes.'

'I'm sure he could beat them all. He's really cheap. And he's really good, a proper artist. Plus he really likes Fieldstar. He could even paint in your logo if you want.' I cringe. Maybe that was going a bit far.

'I do need someone quickly,' he says. He seems more interested now. 'To tell you the truth, the walls here make me want to puke. I was hoping to get it all done before I moved in, but what with the new album and everything . . . Anyway, tell him to pop over later and we'll chat about it.'

Dad is busy on another job but he's always saying he can't afford to turn down work, and I can usually twist him around my little finger. 'Cool,' I say. 'I'll tell him.'

I give Rufus a little wave and practically skip into the hall. There's no sign of Isabella, so I shout 'Bye, then' and let myself out. It's only when I've shut the front door behind me that it strikes me I have completely forgotten about Charlie's football. What a shame. Now I'll *have* to go back and get it.

Chapter 5

Paint Pots and Uggs

'Great news, Dad . . . I've, er, sort of said you'd paint Rufus's house,' I say, nervously, when I come back in. 'I hope you don't mind.' I take a deep breath. 'Oh, and that you'd do it cheap. He wants you to go around with a quote.'

'Ooh, yes,' says Dad, without hesitation. It turns out I don't have to do any twisting – of tales, arms, or around fingers – at all. Dad isn't in the slightest bit angry. Quite the opposite. 'I'd love to,' he says. His other job is practically finished and he's almost as keen as me to meet Rufus.

'Working for a celebrity would be wonderful,' he says.

'My work could end up in one of those *At Home With* features in a magazine. And then, maybe, Mick Jagger will call on my services.'

Mum always calls Dad a 'great big stupid kid' which I suppose he is. But Mum says it like it's a bad thing, which it isn't. Mum was born sensible, born boring, and I can't believe she was ever a kid, let alone a teenager. She probably enjoyed doing her homework and sent herself to bed at nine p.m. with a mug of cocoa and a Latin textbook. How Mum and Dad ever got together is a mystery – and I'd prefer to keep it that way.

'Great, Dad,' I say. 'I think he'll like you.'

When Dad returns from Rufus's house, he looks triumphant. 'I'm starting on Monday,' he announces. 'I'm going to decorate the whole of the downstairs. He loved all of my ideas.'

Mum raises an eyebrow. 'I see,' she says. 'You mean you're charging too little again? Underselling yourself?'

'No,' says Dad. 'I just offered him a better price than his other quotes. Call it mates' rates if you like.' He winks at me.

Mum frowns. 'If he can afford *that* house at today's prices he must be a millionaire,' she says, exasperated. 'He doesn't need a discount. And, anyway, he's not your mate. You've only met him once, about five minutes ago.'

'Spoilsport,' mutters Dad under his breath. 'Well, he might well become a mate. And he already is our next-door neighbour. You never know when you'll need somebody to watch the place or feed the cat when you're on holiday.'

'But we don't have a cat,' says Mum.

'Technicality,' says Dad. 'We might have one, one day.'

'I don't want a cat, I want a dog!' says Charlie. 'Please can we get a dog?'

Mum shakes her head, vigorously. 'Now look what you've done.'

'Pleeeeeeaaaase . . .' cries Charlie.

'No!' says Mum. 'And that's the end of it.'

Charlie sulks and pouts. 'It's not fair,' he says, folding his arms.

'Sorry, little fellow,' says Dad. 'But life's not fair sometimes.'

It's Dad's favourite saying. If life were fair, he often tells me, he'd have his paintings hanging in the Tate Modern and Arsenal would win the Premiership title every year.

When I set off for school on Monday morning, I'm gutted I'm not going to work with Dad instead, to start the decorating at Rufus's house. I've never had any desire to help him before but, suddenly, the idea of carrying buckets of water or helping to strip wallpaper seems strangely appealing.

'I could be your assistant,' I say. It's the third time I've tried this ploy. 'It would be good work experience. Don't you think?'

Dad shakes his head. He promises that I can come along after school for an hour, as long as I make myself useful and do my homework immediately afterwards. Sky, who is still a bit miffed I went and met Rufus without her, can come too, on condition that she also helps, and that we don't bother Rufus. I also invite Vix, who says she might pop in, if she has the time.

I can't think – or talk – about anything else all day. 'So what do you think I should wear?' I ask Vix during lunch break. 'I don't want to get paint on any of my favourite clothes, but I can't go round to Rufus's house wearing my oldest jeans and a baggy top, can I? Especially not when Isabella is likely to walk in at any moment, looking chic and perfect.'

'It doesn't matter,' says Vix. She sounds exasperated. To be fair, I have asked her ten times already. 'You're going to help your dad paint, not going to a gig or a party. You always look nice, anyway.'

'Yeah, I know, but it's *Rufus Justice*. I've seen a lovely painter's smock in the market that would be perfect . . .'

'He might not even be there.'

'He will be,' I say. He'd better be!

I'm out of the school gates the second school ends, like a horse starting the Grand National, but with much glossier hair (I've been coating it with anti-frizz serum all day) and shorter legs. Vix can hardly keep up with me. 'Slow down,' she says. 'I'm getting a stitch!'

'Sorry, Vix. I'm just dying to talk to Rufus again. And I've got to go home, get changed, get over there, help Dad *and* do my homework, all before dinner. Are you sure you don't want to come?'

Vix sighs. 'All right, I'll come for a few minutes. But I won't stay. I'm not sure how Rufus will feel about having half the street in his house.'

'He's used to crowds. He's a rock star, remember. Don't be shy, Vix.'

'I'm not shy.'

It's true, Vix isn't shy – not once you get her talking. She's just quieter than me, or Sky. Less excitable and more thoughtful. That's one of the things that makes her such a good friend.

Half an hour later, Sky, Vix and I are all standing on Rufus's doorstep. I'm wearing my favourite skinny jeans and my birthday party top. It's already decorated in paint-like daubs of colour, which will act like camouflage if I spill any actual paint on it. And, anyway, it's time I bought a new one. Sky is in a clingy jersey dress, while Vix has turned up in her sensible school clothes, which annoys me a little bit, although I don't say anything. It's just that I don't want Rufus to think of us as silly schoolkids.

'Here goes, then,' I say, my finger on the doorbell. The

butterflies in my tummy aren't quite as frantic as last time but I feel shaky at the thought of seeing Rufus again. Sky can hardly contain herself. She's hopping from foot to foot like a toddler who needs the toilet.

The door opens. It's Dad. Sky looks disappointed.

'Hello, girls,' he says. 'Welcome to Chez Rufus.' He leads us into the hall. The entire downstairs of the house is covered with dust sheets, and there are paint pots, brushes and rollers everywhere. 'There's not much for you to do today,' he says. 'You can help me test out some colours on the wall. See what works best.' He checks out our outfits and smirks. 'OK, girls, I've got some overalls you can wear to protect your clothes.'

We hear someone padding down the stairs, and Rufus appears. He's wearing his dressing gown – at four p.m. – and Ugg boots, which looks ridiculous. 'Everything all right, Bob?' he asks. Bob? Nobody calls my dad Bob. He's always Robert, or Robbie, if you're Grandma.

Dad nods. 'It's all going swimmingly, Rufus.' He gestures to us. 'I'd like you to meet my little team of helpers. My daughter Rosie, you've met. These are her friends, Sky and Victoria. They also live on this street.'

Sky gawks at Rufus, open-mouthed. Vix holds out her hand, and Rufus shakes it. 'It's Vix,' she says, smiling.

'Nice to meet you both,' he says. He winks at me and my tummy does a little somersault. 'Right, I'll let you all get on. Have fun, girls.' Then he pads back upstairs again.

'You can close your mouth now, Sky,' I say. 'He's gone.'

'Oh my God,' she says. 'That really *was* Rufus Justice. He's even more gorgeous in the flesh.'

Apart from the Uggs, I think.

Isabella comes out of the kitchen and pops her head around the door. 'Vood you girls like some dreenks?'

'Yes, please,' says Sky, gazing up at her in awe. 'I've got a really dry mouth.'

'Hey, let me help you,' says Vix. She follows Isabella into the kitchen.

About ten minutes later, Vix comes back in, carrying a tray of glasses filled with orange squash and ice cubes. 'I think I'm going to head home now,' she says.

'Already? You were ages,' I say. 'What were you doing?'

'Talking to Isabella.'

'Oh.' I'm surprised. 'What about?'

'She's from the Czech Republic. Remember, I went there on holiday, last year? We were talking about what a beautiful city Prague is, and she was telling me all these places to go, the ones that tourists don't know about.'

'Oh, right.'

'And she was telling me about her work. It was interesting.'

'Is she a model? I guess she must be.'

'No, she hates that – everyone always assumes she is. She's training to be a teacher. She came over here to learn English and got a job as an au pair for someone

Rufus knows. That's how she met him.'

'I didn't realise.'

Vix shrugs. 'She's really nice, actually. You should talk to her.'

'Sure,' I tell her. But I'd much rather talk to Rufus. If I get the chance.

Chapter 6

An Exciting Proposition

Over the next two weeks, I spend at least an hour at Rufus's house every afternoon, and sometimes a couple of hours at the weekend too. Each day, before my eyes, the house is transforming into a pad fit for a rock star, with shiny cream paintwork (some of it, mine), polished floorboards and plush carpets.

I'm surprised at how well Dad and Rufus get on. Surprised and, if I'm honest, a bit jealous. Rufus is always popping in to chat – he doesn't seem to do much when he's at home – but instead of talking to me, he talks to Dad. They share so many interests: art and old cars and music. Rufus likes bands from the Seventies, from way before he was born, the bands that Dad's always trying to get me to listen to. Maybe I should look past the flares and the silly hairstyles and give them a chance.

It's quite difficult to talk to Rufus. We don't have much in common, apart from the fact we both like talking about Rufus Justice. I'm beginning to think he doesn't find me very interesting. He treats me like his kid sister, teasing me and even calling me 'Butterbean' (cringe) or worse, 'Kiddo', which is not how I want to be thought of at all. Not by anyone, but especially not by him. Of course, I don't tell anybody else this. At school, everyone thinks that Rufus and I are practically best mates. I've got a long list of people who want his autograph, which is kind of embarrassing, and even the girls who barely spoke to me before suddenly want to be my friend. People keep asking me for juicy gossip about him too. I always tell them it wouldn't be fair to reveal his secrets but the truth is, I don't know any! Not unless you count the fact he wears Uggs around the house, and that he loves watching stupid quiz programmes on TV. Yes, the biggest surprise about Rufus is that he's turned out to be quite the nerd.

By the end of term, the work is almost finished. There's very little for me to do now, except watch paint dry. Literally. Still, I keep coming round. I can't keep away because I like being part of Rufus's world, even if I'm not really his friend, and I still haven't met the other band members. Plus, I'm angling for tickets to some of the summer festivals. Fieldstar is playing them all this year. Maybe, if I'm really, really good, Mum and Dad will let me go to one of them.

On the very last Saturday of the job, Sky comes with me to see how great the house is looking now. Every room, including the hall, has been plastered, papered and painted and Dad is just applying the finishing touches, adding a fresh coat of paint here, or a brushstroke there. Soon it will be time to hang up the pictures and the mirrors and to put the furniture back. Then Rufus will be able to bring his Wii downstairs again and perch on his favourite sofa, and I won't have any more reasons to come around. Not unless I'm invited, that is.

'Wow, it looks great,' says Sky. 'You wouldn't recognise the place from when you started.'

'I know,' I agree. 'If the Robsons came in the front door now, they'd think they'd got the wrong house.'

'I'm glad you like it,' says Dad, proudly. He puts down his paintbrush and wipes his hands on his overalls. 'Now I'm just going to pop out for a tea break. Back in five.'

'OK, Dad,' I say. I turn to Sky. I've been dying to ask her this . . . 'What the hell *are* you wearing?' She has on this hideous, floaty, peach dress that makes her look both twice as wide as she is and half as tall. 'Didn't your mum give you that for your birthday last year? I thought you hated it.'

'Yes, you're right. I loathe it. It's a monstrosity. Mum asked me why I hadn't worn it lately. So I put it on today, just to please her. Well, that's what she thinks, but really it's because I knew I was coming round here to help. So please, please, please get as much paint, plaster and dirt on it as you can so I won't ever have to wear it out again!'

I giggle. 'Seriously?' I pick up a paintbrush and, tentatively, daub a tiny smudge of red paint on Sky's dress.

'Yes! I mean it! More!'

'OK!' I go over to Dad's toolbox and grab the largest brush I can find. I wave it at Sky, before dunking it into the pot and flicking it as hard as I can. Now there are splotches of red all over her monstrous dress, in her hair, even on her nose. Sky giggles and gets another brush, dipping it into the same pot. She comes at me with the brush, splattering paint across my overalls, and swiping a swatch right across my cheek.

'I can't believe you just did that!' I say. 'This is war!' I take my brush and paint a line straight down the middle of Sky's nose, daubing a bindi-like splot between her eyes.

Sky grins mischievously, and comes at me again, wielding the paintbrush like a knife. She makes two precise stabbing motions at my chest, leaving large, uneven circles on the breast pockets of my overalls. 'Nice nips,' she says. We're laughing so much we can hardly breathe. I think I'm going to wet myself. Sky is doubled over, clutching her tummy. 'It hurts,' she says, panting. 'You look so funny!'

'You should see yourself,' I tell her. 'Ha ha ha ha ha . . . Hell! Oh no! Oh bum!' I've just noticed the wall, the wall that only this morning has been freshly painted in a last coat of cream matt emulsion. Now there are blossom-like splashes of red paint right across it, bleeding downwards to the floor. 'Oh! My! God! Dad's going to kill us! Where's the cream paint? I'd better go over it again, quickly! Or will that just make it go pink? Bum! What shall I do?'

But before I can do anything, Rufus saunters in. 'Nice,' he says, glancing at the walls. 'I especially like the red accents.' He looks at me, and then at Sky, and smiles, wryly. 'They look pretty fetching on you too.' Sky blushes – although it's hard to tell, under all that red paint. 'Your dad didn't mention that idea, but actually, I quite like it. It's very abstract, kind of expressionistic.'

'Really?' I say. I can never tell when Rufus is being sarcastic.

'Yes, if you look at it a certain way it appears almost oriental. Clearly the creative gene runs in your family, Ms Buttery. I think your dad is a creative genius, far too good to be decorating houses. He showed me some of his paintings. I've been thinking about this for a while, but this room has helped make my mind up. When he gets back, I'm going to ask him if he'd like to design our next album cover for us.'

Oh my God. Dad is going to be over the moon. He's always wanted to see his work on the front of an album. He'd prefer it to be on an old style, twelve-inch record, but a CD cover is almost as good. And sometimes Fieldstar do put out their albums on vinyl. 'He'll be dead chuffed,' I say.

'And while you're here, there's something I wanted to ask you too. A favour.'

My tummy lurches. What is he going to ask me? To keep on coming round even when the painting's finished because he'll miss me? To be his stylist? To sing backing vocals with Fieldstar?

'My little brother is coming to stay for the summer holidays,' he says. 'I think he's around the same age as you, probably a bit older. How old are you, again, thirteen?'

That's mortifying. 'I'm fourteen,' I say. I want to add, 'And three-quarters, actually,' but I know that will make me sound even more like a little kid to Rufus.

'Right,' he says. 'Max is fifteen. So that's cool. I wondered if you wouldn't mind looking after him, showing him around and stuff. I thought you could hang out together, take him wherever it is that you and your friends go. Would that be OK?'

Sky shoots me a jealous look. 'You lucky cow,' she mouths.

'Sure,' I say, without hesitation. 'I'd love to.' I'm already picturing Max. I imagine he's a mini version of Rufus, shorter and maybe not quite as muscular, but with the same sharp features, the same unruly mop. Like Rufus, he is bound to be gorgeous and incredibly talented. I can't wait to meet him.

'Cool,' says Rufus. 'Gets him out of my hair, so I appreciate it. He's coming next Saturday afternoon. I'll give you a bell when he arrives.'

Chapter 7

Meeting Max Justice

Max, it turns out, is nothing like Rufus. Nothing at all. He's standing on my doorstep now, a huge grin on his face, looking at me expectantly. I peer at him, studying his features and measuring them against Rufus's using an invisible ruler, the way Dad says he does when he's painting a portrait. They couldn't look more different, which is weird, seeing as they're brothers and must share some DNA. Max has darker eyes and thicker, curlier hair, and his face is rounder, his nose squidgier. Nobody would ever guess they are related. Unless Max is adopted, or Mrs Justice took the wrong baby home from the hospital . . . but that's not something you can ask about on your first meeting with someone, is it? I haven't even said 'hello' yet.

I clear my throat and try not to sound disappointed. 'Oh hi, I'm Rosie.'

He can't tell. He's still grinning inanely at me 'Hi, Rosie, I'm Max. It's great to meet you.'

'Yeah, you too.'

'I like your street.'

'Thanks.' I relax. He seems friendly, warm, easy-going. 'So what do you want to do?' Rufus's only instructions have been to 'look after him for me' – that's six weeks I have to fill, starting right now. 'I could show you the sights or we could just hang out here for a bit. Or go for a coffee, or whatever. Your choice.'

'I want to see Camden Town,' he says. 'I've never been here before. You can give me a guided tour. If that's OK.'

'Sure,' I say, brightening. If there's one thing I know about, it's Camden. 'Where do you want to start?'

'The market, I guess. I've heard it's really cool.'

'Sure,' I say. 'Which one? There's actually six of them . . . I'll show you.' We start to walk. 'You've really never been?' I'm astonished. Hasn't everyone been to Camden Market? It's only one of the biggest tourist attractions in London. When I go on holiday to France or Spain, and I tell people where I'm from, they've always heard of it and they're usually really impressed. 'Where have you been hanging out all this time?'

'Kent,' he says. 'I've been meaning to visit; I've just never got around to it. Although some of my mates have been at weekends. I couldn't wait for Rufus to move down, so I could come and stay.'

We're turning into Camden Road now, passing the takeaways where Mum occasionally allows me to buy dinner, and the newsagent and the skateboard shop and Camden Road railway station, which is hardly ever open because they're always doing engineering works on the line. It's a fine day and the tables outside the Grand Union bar are busy with friends meeting for an early lunch, or a late breakfast. A few metres along is the pharmacy, where most of Mum's patients pick up their prescriptions, and then there's Swanky Hair Design, the hairdresser where Dad gets his hair cut, and where Rufus has – on his recommendation – started going too. It's not unusual to walk past, peer through the glass frontage and see an actor or musician sitting in one of the barber's chairs. I'm not sure if these places are worth pointing out to Max. They're landmarks to me, but probably not of any interest to a visitor. I glance at Max. He's not really looking at the street. He's focusing on me. It makes me feel a bit uncomfortable.

'So how come you're down here for the whole holidays?'

'My parents are going away to Italy for the summer. They've got a villa there. I usually tag along but it gets really boring, and so they said I could stay at Rufus's this

year, now that he's got a proper house with a spare room
– or three.'

'Right,' I say. 'Do you get on well?'

'Yeah, although he's six years older, so it's not like we've
hung out together much. By the time I started secondary
school, he was practically leaving home.'

'I'm a lot older than my brother too,' I tell him. I don't
say that I can't ever imagine wanting to spend my summer
holidays with Charlie. 'Hey, so what's it like having a rock
star as a brother?'

Max shrugs. 'I dunno, he's just Rufus to me. My big
brother. He's been playing in bands ever since I can
remember.'

'Yeah, but it must be weird, seeing him on TV and in
magazines, having groupies around all the time. It must be
exciting.'

'I guess. But I don't know any different, do I? I do get
a bit hacked off when people only want to get to know
me as a way of getting to him. It happens a lot.'

'I bet,' I say, guiltily.

'I can always tell now.'

'Yeah?' Oh God, I think, does he suspect me? Does he
think I'm only spending time with him over the holidays
because he's Rufus's brother? Because that's almost the
truth: I wouldn't have given up my plans so easily for
anyone else. I change the subject, quickly. 'So, er, do you
play in a band?'

'Nah.' Max laughs. 'I had a go on Rufus's drums once, but I was hopeless. Couldn't keep in rhythm. I didn't get anywhere with a guitar, either, even though I had lessons for a while. I guess Rufus got all the musical talent in our family.'

'Oh,' I say. He really is *nothing* like his brother. 'So what do you like doing?'

'Reading graphic novels. And skateboarding.'

'There's a cool skateboard shop I can take you too, just off Camden Road. We passed it a minute ago. And if you head up towards Holloway, there's a skate park too.'

'Yeah, Rufus told me. I can't wait to see it.'

'Hmm, maybe another day,' I say, thinking better of it. I've never been on a skateboard in my life. I tried roller skates once, for a few minutes. Six long weeks later, they finally removed the plaster cast from my arm.

'So what do you like doing?' he asks.

'Listening to music, going to the market, going to gigs – when I'm allowed. That kind of thing. Spending time with my friends mostly. I'll have to introduce you to them.'

'Sure,' says Max. 'That would be nice.'

Now we're coming into Camden Town proper, just approaching the tube station. 'See there,' I say, pointing to my right, at the ugliest building you could imagine. 'That's Sainsbury's. It's hideous, isn't it? But apparently, it was built by some famous architect. I've seen tourists here with guidebooks, taking pictures of it. Weird, huh?'

Max nods. 'I couldn't even tell you what my local supermarket looks like.'

'And there, on your left, is the World's End pub, which is always full of students and, underneath it, The Underworld. Loads of bands play there, especially goth ones.' I'm beginning to enjoy myself now, feeling like a proper tour guide. All I need is one of those big umbrellas, and I could start charging tourists for this . . . 'There's the station . . . We need to cross the road now. Careful . . . This is called Britannia Junction. It's just a crossroads, but it's mentioned in a song by that guy from Blur. That's the Electric Ballroom, another venue.'

'Hasn't Rufus played there?'

'Yeah, that's right. A couple of years ago, before Fieldstar got really big. I was too young to go then. Ah, here's where the market starts. This is actually called Camden Market, it's the modern bit. It's good for T-shirts and stuff. Want to look?'

'Sure,' says Max. 'If it's OK with you. I could do with a new T-shirt.'

'Course. You'd better stick close. It's really crowded.'

'Will do,' says Max. He grins at me.

We walk around slowly, stopping to pause at the occasional stall. They're all selling the same things: T-shirts emblazoned with band names and logos, old leather jackets and jewellery from India. 'The other markets are better, I think,' I say, apologising. But Max seems really excited, even a bit overwhelmed. I think it's sweet. I've forgotten what it's like to see Camden with fresh eyes. I have to remind myself that most people have boring high streets, with the same old chain stores and mobile phone shops. Of course, Camden has those too, but they're mostly the other way, towards Mornington Crescent.

'What do you think of that T-shirt?' he asks. He's pointing to a stall selling tops with comic book heroes on them. 'The blue Judge Dredd one that's hanging at the front?'

I don't have a clue who Judge Dredd is, and I don't much like the T-shirt Max has chosen (it's got a weird man with a mask on it), but I'm not going to tell him that. 'Looks good,' I say. 'How much?'

'Only a fiver. I think I'm going to get it.' He asks the stallholder to fetch it down for him so he can try it on, then goes behind a makeshift curtain to undress. He comes out a few seconds later, wearing the T-shirt. It's a bit big for him, but he doesn't seem to mind. 'What do you think, Rosie?'

'It looks great.' It does suit him. I wait while he pays. 'Shall we move on up the road?'

Max nods, enthusiastically. I can tell he's having a good time by the way he's swinging his arms and humming softly to himself as he walks along.

'Hey, Max . . .' I gesture to my right. 'That's where the big fire was, a couple of years ago. It started in that pub where all the celebs go. You could see the flames and smoke from my house. It was a bit scary, especially when they thought the gas canisters were going to blow up. We nearly got evacuated.'

'Yeah, I remember. It was on the news.'

'My dad thinks it was dodgy. He says someone started it deliberately so they could redevelop the land. There's a new market there now. Maybe we'll look at that one another time, when we go down to the canal? I'll take you to the Lock bit, and the Stables market now. They're the best ones.'

'OK,' says Max. 'I'd like that.'

We pass shop after shop selling shoes and second-hand clothes, past cafés and restaurants and pubs, where bands are playing live. The tunes and beats bleed out into the street, getting all mixed up together into one big mess of noise. I've always thought it's like a soundtrack for Camden Town. Max seems overwhelmed by the shop fronts, which are all painted in vibrant colours – some of them even have giant models of boots or skulls or even aeroplanes on their roofs – and by the crowds of people we're weaving through. There are punks with stripy mohicans, Rastafarians with dreadlocks, goths in corsets and pale make-up, and indie kids in sprayed-on skinny jeans and eyeliner. Just like the music, all mixed up together, happily. Nobody looks out of place in Camden Town. I once saw a guy walking down the street with his pants over his trousers – like Superman. No one gave him a second glance.

We walk under the railway bridge, where Camden High Street meets Chalk Farm Road, and now we're at the Lock Market, just a few metres from the Stables Market.

'What's that smell?' says Max, sniffing suspiciously.

I giggle. 'What do you think it is?'

'No! People smoke weed here, in the street?'

'Yeah,' I tell him. I'm so used to it, I've forgotten how surprising it is to most people. 'And down by the canal. The police are always cracking down, and they have sniffer dogs at the station sometimes. But give it a few weeks and everything goes back to normal.'

Max widens his eyes. 'You live in the maddest place,' he says.

'I suppose I do. But it's all I've ever known.' A bit, I think, like taking it for granted that your brother is a rock star. 'Hey, are you hungry?'

'I kind of am. Is there somewhere good round here?'

'Ha! You could say that. Follow me.' I lead him into the market, through a maze of stalls. 'Now take your pick.' On either side of us, for as far as you can see, are food stalls serving every cuisine imaginable. On sale here are veggie-burgers, falafel in pitta bread, home-made cakes, Italian ice cream and even Polish delicacies. There are organic hot dog vendors and stalls selling smoked salmon sandwiches. Alongside them stand Moroccan stalls serving up couscous and tagines, and Chinese vendors dishing up noodles and stir fries. If you prefer something a little spicier, there are Indian curries or Mexican chillies. And, if you're a health nut, you can have a salad, with orange juice squeezed freshly before your eyes. All of the stallholders are competing for our attention as we pass, trying to shout louder than the person on the stall next to them: 'Wanna try? Wanna try?'

'Wow,' says Max. 'Too much choice. Some chicken noodles, maybe?'

'Sounds good,' I say. 'I think I'll have the same.'

'Let me get these. My treat. To say thank you for showing me around today.'

'Really? If you're sure? Thanks, Max.'

We sit on a step and slurp our noodles, chatting about our friends and what we like doing after school. I wouldn't usually eat noodles (or spaghetti) with a guy because they're far too messy and I'd be self-conscious. But I'm not trying to impress Max, so it doesn't really matter if I splash a bit of sauce on my top or if it dribbles down my chin. I feel comfortable with him, like I do with my girlfriends. He's so much easier to talk to than Rufus: more down to earth, less up himself.

After we eat, we wander around the market for a while longer. I take Max to see the antique stalls and the furniture shops, where you can buy space-age sofas from the Sixties, shaped like swings or giant red lips. I show him the best vintage clothes shops and I let him hunt for back issues of his favourite graphic novels in the second-hand bookshops. By now, we're both starting to feel tired. There's just too much to see, too much noise and too many colours.

'We can come back another time,' I say, after I've suggested we head home. 'You really can't do it all in one day. It's too much.'

'Yeah, it's total sensory overload,' he agrees. 'But I've had an ace time.'

'Me too,' I say. And I really mean it. As we walk home, I think how good it will be to have a new guy friend to hang out with for the summer. I can't wait to introduce him to Sky and Vix.

Chapter 8

The Celebrity Dinner Party

I wake up smiling. Which doesn't happen very often. Usually, I feel grumpy, but I've slept for almost twelve hours and I feel great. School broke up on Friday, the day before Max arrived, so not only is it the first official day of the summer holidays, which means I don't have to go to school today, tomorrow or for as far ahead as I can imagine, but I also had *the* best night, last night. Yesterday, soon after we'd come home from the market, Max rang to ask me if I'd like to have dinner at Rufus's later. I didn't take too much persuading. In a contest between dinner with a rock star and Mum's 'cooking', there could only ever be one winner. Dad was rather keen on coming too — despite his lack of an invitation – although he claimed it was only because he wanted to show Rufus the sketches he'd been working on for the album cover. 'You'll have to show him another time,' I told him, firmly. 'Tonight is just for young people.'

I thought I was going round for a casual bite to eat, but it turned out to be a proper, grown-up dinner party, like the ones my parents have, except with much cooler guests. A couple of Rufus's musician friends were there (no one else from Fieldstar, unfortunately), and Isabella had invited one of her Czech friends, another au pair named Ivana, who was almost as beautiful and even taller than her. I couldn't help wondering if they were manufactured on a production line, like Barbie dolls. Ivana didn't speak much English, so she and I grinned at each other a lot and waved our hands around.

I pull the duvet up over my chin and lie still for a few minutes, thinking how I can't wait to tell Sky and Vix all about it, and how envious they'll be. I was at Rufus's until past eleven-thirty, until Mum texted me (for the third time) to say I *had* to come home and go to bed, even if it was the summer holidays. Spoilsport. Everything about last night was brilliant, including the food. I mean, I didn't think I liked fish, unless it came coated in batter with a side order of chunky chips, but Isabella's fish dish was delicious. I would have asked for seconds, if I hadn't thought I'd look greedy.

'This is divine,' I said. 'Er, what is it?'

'Eez sea bass,' said Isabella. 'Wiz lemongrass and ginger and crushed po-ta-toes.'

'Isn't it good?' said Rufus, licking his lips. 'It's amazing that someone from a landlocked country has such a wicked way with our scaly friends, eh?' He looked proudly at Isabella and put his arm around her.

'Yes, absolutely,' I agreed, although I had no idea what he was talking about. It was only when I got home and googled it, that I learned that the Czech Republic doesn't have a coast. The whole evening was like that: people discussing things I knew nothing about – politics and obscure bands and places I'd never visited – but including me in the conversation, so I didn't feel left out. Even Rufus was much friendlier to me than he'd been before. He told me all about what life was like on a Fieldstar tour: sleeping in a cramped, smelly bus and spending such a short time in each place that, after a few days, you can't work out which country you're in. He told me how dull it was to make a pop video and go to the Brit Awards, even though it might look glamorous, and what a buzz it was to play live in Hyde Park with thousands of people singing along with you. He said how pleased he was that I was getting on with Max so well, and that I must come for dinner again. He even let Max and me have one small glass of wine each. Of course, I lied and said I drink wine all the time at home, and so my parents wouldn't mind at all. It tasted foul and made my head swim, but I still drained the whole glass.

After dinner, we all went into the living room (nobody said anything about the walls I'd painted), and sat chatting over coffee. Rufus's friend brought out his guitar for an impromptu jamming session and everyone – even Max – joined in, singing Fieldstar songs and old tunes too.

Just thinking about it now makes me smile. I rub my eyes and look around me. There are Fieldstar posters all over my bedroom walls, including one directly above my bed, one in which Rufus isn't wearing a top. When I look at it now, I feel slightly embarrassed, dirty even, like I'm perving on a relative. Eughh. There he is, flexing his muscles and pouting in a way I have never seen him pout. Come to think of it, I've never seen anybody pout like that in real life. I study my other posters. Rufus does look different in the pictures. He looks blank, vacant, as if he's not really there. All the hours I've spent gazing at these posters, staring into his eyes, trying to work out what he was thinking, and it turns out he wasn't thinking anything at all. Except, probably, 'When will this be over so I can go home and play on my Wii?'

Max is coming over later to hang out and meet Sky and Vix. I really need to do something about my bedroom first. There's no way I can let Max come in when there are photos of his big brother on every wall. It's just too weird. I stretch, climb out of bed and put on a T-shirt and trackie bottoms. 'Right,' I say aloud. 'Time to get to work.' I stand up on tiptoes on my bed and, in one swift move, rip down the picture of Rufus's torso. Perhaps I'm a little too hasty, because it tears, severing one of his arms from his body. Ouch. Lucky I'm not superstitious, because I'm sure that can't be a good omen for a drummer. Then, one by one, I peel the Fieldstar posters from my walls. They've been up there for about a year now, and the blu-tack leaves marks on the paintwork. I stop to see how I'm doing. The room looks bare, dull, characterless. I've had posters up for as long as I can remember, ever since dad painted over the alphabet wallpaper for me. It was a rush job and I can still make out faint traces of letters in the spots where the paint has rubbed away. I can't leave it like that; I'll have to find some other posters to replace them.

There's no time to go to the market, so I hunt around my room for anything I can use. Tucked under my bed is a rolled-up cardboard tube that I'd forgotten about. Inside it there are several posters. I unfurl them: there's the cute kitten I used to gaze at from my bed when I was about seven, a Disney film poster for *Beauty and the Beast*, a picture of Westlife from years ago, that I didn't have the heart to throw away, and a portrait that I picked up in the market cheap, of a cute guy with dark, curly hair and a beret-type hat. I meant to put it up when I bought it, but there wasn't room for it before. Now, there is. I paste it up above my bed, where Rufus used to pout, topless. It looks good, like it fits. But the room still looks wrong somehow, not like mine, so I stick the other posters up too. It's all a bit of a hotch-potch — more like the poster section of IKEA than a room that someone real lives in — but at least you can't see the marks on the walls any more, or the traces of the alphabet wallpaper.

Right, I've got one hour till my friends arrive. I need to shower and dress and try to eat some breakfast, even though it's lunchtime already, and I'm still full from last night. Mmm, that chocolate pudding was divine . . . the way the rich, hot sauce oozed out when I touched it with my spoon. I *did* ask for seconds of that!

I am just about ready when the doorbell rings. If I'm lucky, it will be either Sky or Vix, or both of them together, so I can fill them in on last night before Max arrives. But it's him.

'Hi,' he says, grinning again. He kisses me on the cheek. I can't help noticing that he's wearing aftershave — the same scent that Rufus uses. He must have borrowed it. 'It's really good to see you again.'

It's only been about fourteen hours, but I play along. 'Why, did you miss me?'

'Course,' he says. I might be wrong, but I think his neck and ears turn slightly red. 'Did you have a good time last night?'

'Oh yes, it was brilliant. Come in.' I lead him into the hall. 'I had so much fun. Rufus and his friends were lovely and, now I've spent a bit of time with her, I really like Isabella too. I didn't think I would at first.'

'Yeah, she's fab. And she's good for Rufus. She keeps him out of trouble.'

'Trouble?'

'You know, hanging out with dodgy people, falling out of

nightclubs and ending up in the papers. He went through a phase of that. It wasn't really like him at all. I think the fame went to his head a bit.'

'Yeah, I remember,' I say. I'm glad Rufus isn't like that any more; there's no way my parents would let me hang out with him if they heard those stories. 'Come upstairs. We can wait for the others in my room.'

Max follows me up the stairs and into my bedroom, perching himself on the edge of my bed. I sit down next to him, not too close, and cross my legs.

'So what do you have planned for me today?' he says, looking around him. He's obviously taking in the strange decor, but he doesn't say anything.

'Not sure. I thought we'd wait till the others get here and see what they want to do.'

'OK. Whatever it is, I hope it's as fun as yesterday.'

'It will be, I promise. Sky and Vix are my oldest, bestest mates. They can't wait to meet you.'

'Sure,' he says, although he doesn't sound as keen to meet them as I'd expect. 'It'll be nice.'

Vix and Sky arrive together; they've probably met up on the street outside. Max waits in my room, while I go downstairs to open the door. We're all dying to have a good gossip, but sound carries through my house, and I don't want Max to hear us talking about him. 'He's here already – upstairs,' I whisper. 'Tell you later.'

He's standing waiting for us by the bedroom door when

we come in. 'Hi,' he says, politely, holding out his hand. Vix shakes it and says, 'Nice to meet you.' Sky nods and leans over to give him a peck on the cheek.

'So . . .' I say. There's an awkward silence. Everyone is looking at my bedroom walls and I just know someone is going to say something.

'Interesting new posters,' says Sky, smirking. 'I didn't know you were into Westlife again.'

'Well, I fancied a change,' I say, making a face at Sky, who must have guessed why I've taken down my Fieldstar pictures. When I'm sure Max can't see, I mouth 'Shush' at her.

'Yeah, but since when have you been into Che Guevara?' asks Vix, staring at the new poster above my bed.

'Who?'

'The guy on your wall up there.'

'Oh, yeah, right. Shayne what? I picked that up in the market ages ago. How do you know him? Is he an actor?'

Vix giggles. 'Not exactly.'

'I didn't know you were an old commie,' says Sky.

'Eh?'

'Che Guevara was a Cuban Marxist revolutionary,' says Vix. 'In the Fifties. Didn't you know?'

I turn beetroot. 'I think I've heard of him, but I didn't realise what he looked like,' I say quietly. 'I just thought he was a cute guy. I wondered why there were so many pictures of him in Camden Market. Whoops.'

'Oh, Rosie,' says Vix. She laughs at me, but not unkindly. 'I suppose he was.'

'Rosie's not really into politics or history, are you, Rosie?' says Sky, teasing.

'She knows about a lot of other things though,' says Max, sweetly sticking up for me. 'She gave me the best guided tour of Camden yesterday.'

'Course she did,' says Vix. 'She's great, really, is our Rosie.'

'Hey, everyone, I am here, you know!' I say. 'So what do you all want to do today?' I change the subject, before anyone can say anything about the Disney poster, or the cute kitten. I've had enough humiliation for one day.

'How about a picnic in Primrose Hill?' suggests Vix. 'It's such a lovely day.'

'Genius idea! Why doesn't everyone go home, grab some food and drinks and we can meet at the end of the road in, say, twenty minutes?'

Chapter 9
A-Listers
and Beansprouts

Primrose Hill is as close as you can get to a village in London. It's the posh area, right next to Camden Town, about a twenty-minute walk from my house. Primrose Hill is picture-perfect, with old-fashioned street lamps and red telephone boxes outside huge, Victorian houses – the way London looks in movies. It's full of expensive boutiques, restaurants and delicatessens, and yummy mummies pushing prams or driving their children to private schools in four-by-fours. This is where the really famous, really rich people live, the people who find Camden Town too seedy, or too noisy. It's not unusual to see a Hollywood star here, taking his children for a walk, or buying an organic loaf at the bakery.

The hill itself backs on to Regent's Park and is a steep climb, which really gets your legs. But it's worth it. If you walk up one of the paths to the top you can see almost the whole of London spreading out before you, panoramically: the BT Tower, the Millennium Wheel, even as far as the Dome and the skyscrapers of Canary Wharf. I love going there with my friends on Sundays and summer holiday afternoons, to hang out and listen to our iPods.

It's also the perfect place for a picnic. We've all packed ingredients from our kitchens that can be cobbled together into a picnic of sorts: crisps and chocolate, some fruit and leftover pasta salad. Sky's brought some weird concoction with beansprouts and tofu that her mum found in the health food shop. It stinks.

'Shall I toss it?' she asks, as we pass a bin on Chalk Farm Road, just before the tube station.

I look at Sky, who looks at Vix, who looks at Max, who looks back at me, and we all nod. 'Yes please!' I say. I know some people are starving but, honestly, I've seen tramps put Sky's mum's food back in the bin.

Our arms linked together in a chain, we walk up the steep hill that leads to the railway bridge, which marks the entrance to Primrose Hill village. Vix suggests that we go into the grocery store to buy a couple of bottles of Coke and a few extras to supplement our picnic. It's crazily expensive in there – twice the price of Sainsbury's – but they always have the tastiest treats, and if everyone puts in a couple of pounds, it's not so bad.

We're standing in the queue to pay when Sky squeals 'Oh my God!' just as a tall guy wearing sunglasses walks past us along the aisle. She whispers, rather too loudly, 'Isn't that Adam Grigson again? Quick, Rosie, it's Celebometer time!'

'Yes, well done Sky! I think it is.' My pulse speeds up with excitement. 'What's he doing this time?'

Sky peers over the shelves. 'It looks like he's buying a newspaper and some cheese. It's Brie. No, Camembert.'

'Celeb-what?' says Max, intrigued.

'Celebometer,' says Vix. Maybe I'm being paranoid, but she sounds a bit condescending. 'Rosie has invented this celebrity-spotting game. You get points depending on how famous someone is. Oh, and how hot they are.'

'It's nothing,' I say. 'Honestly.' Celebrity spotting feels wrong in front of Max. After what he told me, I don't want him to think I'm shallow and fake, like the people who try to befriend him to meet his brother.

'Oh right, I see,' says Max, who clearly can't tell I'm embarrassed. 'So how many points do you get for Adam Grigson, then? Because I've just seen Robert De Niro walk past the shop.'

'Seriously?' My voice leaps about ten octaves.

'No,' says Max. 'Not really.' He laughs. 'But you should have seen the look on your face. Classic!'

I slap him on the arm. 'You're mean.'

'Yeah, and you're gullible.'

We wander into the park and find a shady spot, halfway up the hill, just under a tree. Vix has brought a blanket, which she spreads out on the grass, and we all sit down on it, using our jackets as cushions. Then we pile our food into the middle and tuck in happily, sharing around the crisps and the little cupcakes we bought in the grocery store. After we've eaten, we lie down in a circle across the blanket, with our feet virtually touching, and play silly word association games and I-spy. Max swears that he's spotted a UFO, but it turns out to be just an aeroplane, zigzagging its way through the clouds, on its flight path into Heathrow.

'Will you walk up to the top of the hill with me, Rosie?' he asks, when the game has fizzled out and nobody can be bothered to start a new one.

'Course,' I say, clambering up. 'Will you two be all right for a few minutes?'

Vix and Sky are still lying down, their eyes closed. 'Sure,' murmurs Sky, sleepily. 'Have fun.'

Max and I trudge up the hill together. It's hard to believe that I've only known him for a couple of days, because it feels like for ever. And I'm so pleased he's getting on well with Sky and Vix, and that they seem to like him too. He's just slotted in, as if he's always been a member of the gang. Hanging out with him for the rest of the summer won't be a bind at all. It will be fun.

'What an amazing view,' he says, at the top, a little out of breath. 'It's like looking at a postcard of London.'

'I know,' I say. 'That's probably why they've made so many films up here.' I pause to take in the view myself. 'If you look down there, to your left, you can see the zoo. See that high bit – that's the aviary, where the birds live. I'll have to show you it properly one day. It's dead expensive to get in the main entrance, but if you walk round the back, along the canal, you can see some of the animals for free.'

'I wish I lived in London,' says Max. 'As soon as I'm old enough, I'm going to move here.'

'You should,' I say.

We stand and look for a while longer before heading back down the hill to sit on the blanket with the others and chat. Max tells us about his school; it's a boarding school, but he comes home every weekend. Rufus went there too. It's no ordinary school: the pupils make the rules themselves, which sounds bizarre – not to mention extremely appealing. Why can't my school be like that?

'So you can choose whether to go to lessons?' asks Vix.

'Yeah, sort of. If I wanted to, say, go on a trip to a museum, instead of going to a history lesson, that would be OK. And there's loads of drama and music and social stuff, which they think is just as important as academic work. It's all about making you "a well-rounded person", apparently. Most people end up with really good exam results in the end, so we must do some work, I guess. Loads of famous people went there. Not just Rufus.'

'God, sign me up!' says Sky. She fills Max in on what it's like at her comprehensive. 'I bet you a million pounds it would be empty every day if we could choose whether to go to lessons or not.'

'Are there girls at your school, Max?' asks Vix.

'Yeah, it's totally mixed. I've got loads of girl mates.'

That figures, I think. It must be why he's so relaxed in our company. Some of the boys I know treat me like I'm a strange creature from another planet. 'Me and Vix go to a girls' school,' I tell him. 'Although we do have some boys in the sixth form.'

'Yeah,' says Vix. 'So do you have a girlfriend?' It's not like her to be so direct, and she blushes a little.

'No, I was seeing someone last year, but it didn't work out. What about all of you?'

'Not me,' says Vix. 'I'm single. So is Rosie. But Sky's got a boyfriend.'

'Sort of,' says Sky. 'It's a bit shaky at the moment. I'm not really sure where I stand.' She looks sad.

'Sorry to hear that. Anyway . . .' says Max, immediately changing the subject.

So he is a typical guy, in some ways. None of them like talking about feelings, or relationships, especially tortured ones like Sky's.

'I'd actually better be going.' He drags himself up from the ground and brushes grass and twigs from his jeans. 'I promised Rufus I'd help him set something up on his PC this evening, and I'm already later than I said I'd be.'

'Are you sure you know your way back on your own?' asks Vix. 'I'm going to have to go home myself, soonish, so I could walk you back.' She moves as if to get up to join him, climbing to her knees. But her leg is dead from sitting on it too long and she virtually topples over.

'Oh no, don't worry, stay there. I'll be fine,' he says, smiling at me. 'I've got inbuilt GPS. But if I get lost, I'll call.'

'OK,' says Vix, who seems disappointed. She sits back down again, rubbing the life back into her leg.

Max says his goodbyes and we watch him silently, as he makes his way down the hill and out through the park gate, where he disappears from view.

'So, now he's gone, what do we all think of Max?' I say. 'I've been dying to ask you. He's all right, isn't he?'

'I like him,' says Sky. 'He's a nice guy. Fun. A bit posh, but down-to-earth. You'd never guess he was Rufus's brother though, would you?'

I shake my head. 'No way! I told you.'

'I think he's lovely,' says Vix. She sighs. '*Really* lovely.'

'Vix!' says Sky. 'Have you got a bit of a crush? It's not like you.'

'Maybe a little,' says Vix. 'But I doubt he'll like me back. He doesn't seem remotely interested. Anyway, did you see the way he was looking at Rosie the whole time, grinning like the cat who —'

'Don't be silly,' I interrupt. 'We're just mates. It's probably just because he knows me better than you two.'

'You think? So you're not interested?' asks Vix.

'Nah, I don't think so,' I say.

If I were, I'd know, wouldn't I?

Chapter 10

How Do You Know If You Fancy Someone?

It's a few days later, and I'm on my way to the high street when I see Rufus, standing in the middle of the road outside the art collective house. For some reason, he's staring up at the roof but, as far as I can tell, there's nothing there.

'Hey, Rufus, what are you doing?' I say. I'm still a bit nervous about starting conversations with him, but if I just think of him as Max's big brother and not as the celeb next door, it's much easier.

He turns around and smiles, as if he's actually pleased to see me. 'Ah, Rosie, hello. I was on my way to check out the collective. One of the guys invited me along. Want to come with?'

'Ooh yes,' I say. I've been dying to see what goes on inside the collective's house ever since the artists moved in. (Do squatters *move* in or break in?) Plus, Mum would go ballistic if she knew, which makes it even more appealing.

'Come on, then,' he says. He begins to stride towards the front door, with me a couple of steps behind him. I have to run a little to catch up.

'Why were you looking up at the roof like that?'

'Ah,' he says. 'Well, if you want to get into the art collective, you have to follow a secret code. They told me to stand here, wait and look up. One of them appeared at the top left-hand window and made a hand signal when it was safe for me to come in.'

'Wow,' I say. 'Seriously? I didn't see anyone.'

'No,' says Rufus. 'Don't be silly. I just have to ring the doorbell like at any other house. I was looking up at the sky because I thought I heard a helicopter.'

I blush. This is just the sort of wind-up Max would pull on me. Rufus raises his left eyebrow and grins at me, mischievously, and for the first time I can see a little of his brother in him.

'I did know you were joking, obviously,' I say.

'Sure you did.' He sounds unconvinced. 'Don't worry, Max tells me you've got a wicked sense of humour. Among other things. He probably won't thank me for telling you this, but he likes you, you know.'

'Oh, that's great. I really like him too. He's good to hang out with.'

'Hmm,' says Rufus. 'And?'

'What do you mean?'

'Is that all? You just like hanging out?'

'I don't get you?'

'God, Rosie, you are slow today. He *likes* you.'

'Oh,' I exclaim, as what he means finally dawns on me. I know I look OK from certain angles, but I never expect anyone to think I'm attractive. 'You don't mean . . .'

'You got it, Ms Buttery. Max has got the hots for you. He fancies you.' He grins again, cheekily. 'So, my little brother and you, eh? What do you think?'

'I . . . I . . . don't know,' I begin, flustered. The first thing that pops into my head to say is, 'Max is lovely, but I don't like him like that,' but the truth is I'm not really sure how I feel. I love hanging out with Max, but I don't know him well enough yet to know if I fancy him. Which is a rubbish excuse, because that's never made a difference before. Usually, when I fancy someone, I don't have to think about it: I just look at them and I know, instantly. But maybe I could fancy Max. He's such a great guy . . . maybe he will grow on me. None of my other boyfriends (OK, there's only been two of them) has ever worked out, have they? So maybe having butterflies in your tummy when you look at someone is actually a bad thing, and it's good that I don't get them when I'm with Max.

And then there's Vix – Vix, who hardly ever fancies anyone but who has made it clear she's interested in Max. If anything happens between me and Max, she'll be upset, won't she? Things are already a bit weird between us. But if he likes me, not her, then there's not much either of us can do about it, is there? It would be pointless to throw away my chance just so I don't hurt her. And it's not as if Vix has declared her undying love for Max; she's just said she might have a little crush. She's only spent a few hours with him, after all, and I introduced him to her. She can hardly say, 'I bagsied him first.' Max isn't a pair of shoes in a shop window, he's a person. Oh, boo, it's all so complicated. How I wish there were rules about these things.

'Yes?' says Rufus, raising his left eyebrow, and I wonder if he can see the cogs turning in my brain.

'Um . . . tell him I *might* do,' I say, cryptically.

'Ah, playing hard to get,' says Rufus. 'I like your style. I'll let him know.'

I give him a coy smile. That isn't it, at all, but I'm not going to let him know how confused I am.

'Right,' he says. 'Let's check out the collective.' He rings the doorbell, without waiting for me to reply. It takes an age for someone to answer, but then there's the sound of several locks being turned, and a girl peeps her head around the door. She has enormous green eyes and she would be very pretty if she didn't have half her head shaved and piercings in her eyebrow, nose and lip.

'Hi there,' says Rufus. 'I've brought a little friend, Rosie, with me, I hope that's OK.'

Oh my God, Rufus Justice called me his friend! I'm not quite so keen on the 'little' part, but I'll forgive it. I grin at the girl, revelling in my new status.

'Sure,' she says, looking me up and down, suspiciously. 'Hi, I'm Amanda.' She lets us in and I stop for a second, taking in the decor. The inside of the collective house looks like any other house on the street, except the floorboards are bare, there are empty wine bottles and beer cans everywhere, and the unpapered walls are covered in doodles and half-finished paintings. Some of the paintings seem very familiar in style. There's this famous but mysterious artist known as Winksy, who paints images on walls in the dead of night, and there have been several rumours that he lives in Camden. Could these paintings be his? Does he live here? Am I going to meet him? Wait till I tell Dad . . .

'Rufus, Jack is waiting for you in the rehearsal room just here,' says Amanda, pointing to her left. 'Rosie, why don't I show you around?'

'OK,' I say, keen to explore. I turn to say goodbye to Rufus, but he's already disappeared.

'So how do you know Rufus?' asks Amanda.

I wonder if I should make up an intriguing story, but I can't think of anything. 'Er, he lives next door.'

Amanda bristles. 'Oh right. I thought I'd seen you around. Well, please don't tell anyone on the street about what you find here. The council is trying to get us out.'

'I know,' I say. 'It sucks.' I don't tell her that Mum, as chairperson of the residents' association, is backing them all the way.

Amanda doesn't talk much as she shows me around; she just opens doors and points at things, like she can't wait to get it over with. The collective house is amazing. They've got darkrooms for photography, art rooms that Dad would kill for, and music studios. There's also a huge space for parties, where there are decks permanently set up, which extends out into the garden and is covered by a canopy. Amanda doesn't show me where anyone sleeps, and I think it would be rude to ask, but I'm dying to see. She does tell me there are up to fifteen people living here at any one time. I wonder what she'd say if I asked to move in for a while . . .

'Right,' says Amanda. 'Tour over. Sorry, but the rest is private and I've got stuff to do.'

'Oh,' I say, disappointed. I want to stay longer, to meet some of the others, especially if one of them might be Winksy. Everyone I've passed looks really quirky and interesting. One guy was dressed like he'd stepped out of a photo from the Forties, complete with a moustache and RAF flying jacket.

It's not to be. Amanda shows me to the front door. 'Nice to meet you,' she says. 'See you around.' No party invite, or suggestion to return. She opens the door just wide enough so that I can squeeze through the gap and bolts it shut behind me. Before I walk away, I stand on the doorstep for a moment, wondering if I'll ever have the chance to go inside again.

What to do about Max bugs me all afternoon. I'm glad I'm not seeing him today – he's gone to meet some friends from school who live in South London. When he sends me a text to find out how I am, I reply with a friendly message but I feel really self-conscious about putting three kisses at the end, even though I always do that. Funny how knowing someone fancies you changes everything. I wonder if Rufus has told him what I said yet? I feel like I need to talk about it, but Sky isn't picking up her phone, and obviously I can't talk to Vix. Dad is home, so I decide to ask him for his opinion. He can be quite good at giving advice because he doesn't see life like most older people do; he still remembers being a teenager and what it feels like.

Dad is in his studio, surrounded by sketchbooks and screwed up bits of paper with half-finished drawings on them. He looks frustrated. He tells me he's having another go at the Fieldstar album cover. Rufus didn't like his first ideas because he said they weren't 'honest' enough, whatever that means. The problem is, he won't let Dad hear the tracks (they still haven't been mastered) or tell him what the new album is called, mainly because it doesn't have a name yet. 'We're trying to come up with something that truly captures the genuine nature of the material,' he told Dad. As Fieldstar's first two albums were called *Fieldstar* and *Fieldstar Two*, it's probably not too much of a stretch to guess the title of the third one, but that doesn't really help Dad.

'Can I ask you something, Dad?' I say, cautiously.

'Of course you can, Rosie. You can ask me anything you like – as long as it's not for a bigger monthly allowance.'

'No, no. It's nothing like that. It's personal.'

Dad stiffens. I think he looks a trifle scared, as if he's going to have to give me a lecture on the birds and the bees, or something. 'Are you sure you don't want to ask your mother? She's better on *that* kind of thing.'

'No, really, she isn't. And don't worry, it's not a woman thing. It's a life thing.'

He relaxes. 'OK. Fire away.'

I'm not sure how to explain myself, so I just come straight out with it. 'How do you know when you fancy someone? I mean, how can you be sure?'

Dad creases his brow. 'Hmm, I think you just know.'

This is what I'm afraid of. 'Yeah, but is it always right away?'

'Oh, no,' says Dad, a misty look in his eyes. 'It can take time. One day you don't notice someone – they're just a friend, or a colleague – and then they say something, or do something, or wear something, and you look at them and you think they're the most beautiful, perfect person you've ever seen, and you can't imagine ever not feeling that way.'

'Really?'

'Oh yes. When I first clapped eyes on your mother, I wasn't interested in her romantically at all. I thought she was a bit bossy, a bit prim. And she used to wear these horrible, shapeless black dresses, although to be fair, it was the Eighties . . . Don't ever tell her I told you this, but it was her friend Susie I was after . . .'

'Too. Much. Information.'

He doesn't take any notice. In his mind he's gone back twenty-five years, and he's at university, falling in love with my mother. '. . . But one day, in my third year, I bumped into her in the university canteen — literally, bumped into her — and then she spilled coffee all over herself, and the expression on her face made me melt. She looked like she wanted to kill me . . .'

'La la la la la la la la . . .' I have my hands over my ears now.

'And after that, I couldn't stop thinking about her. And then,' he winks, 'I invited her to come and see my etchings . . .'

'Stop it! Please! You're torturing me.'

He laughs at me. 'Sorry, Rosie. But you'll be forty-five one day too and nostalgic for your youth.'

'No I won't,' I say. 'That's never going to happen to me. And if it does, I think I'll kill myself first. Anyway, it's taking long enough to get to fifteen.'

He sighs and rubs the back of my head. I grimace – I've told him not to do that because it makes my hair frizz. 'Oh, Rosie, my love.'

I duck away from him. 'So, getting back to what I asked, if you don't fancy someone the minute you see them, it doesn't mean you never will?'

'That's right. So why are you asking? Who's the lucky fella?'

'No one,' I say. 'I was just wondering.'

'OK.' He looks hurt that I won't tell him, like he thinks I don't trust him.

I pause. 'If you really want to know, it's Max, Rufus's brother. Rufus told me he likes me and I don't know if I like him back. Like that, I mean. I'm kind of enjoying having a guy friend.'

Dad smiles, kindly. 'Don't rush into anything, love. Just because he's a guy and he likes you doesn't mean you have to go out with him. You can stay just as you are. It's perfectly possible to be platonic friends.'

'Yeah, but I don't want to hurt his feelings. He might not even want to be my friend any more if I knock him back. It would spoil everything.'

'It's a tricky one. If it makes any difference, both your mum and I think Max is a very nice young man. We wouldn't have any objections.'

'Daaaad!' I cringe. 'Is that like a reverse psychology thing? If you say you like him, you hope you'll put me off?'

'Course not. I know you're far too clever for that to work.'

'Hmm. There's another thing: Vix fancies him. She actually said so.'

'Oh, yes, I can see that is awkward.' He ponders my dilemma for a moment. 'But you know what they say, Rosie? All's fair in love and war. I'm sure you're all going to have lots of boyfriends along the way. If you're good friends, you won't let them come between you.'

I nod. Dad hasn't really told me anything I didn't already know, or helped me to make my mind up, but I do feel a bit better.

Later, Sky pops round to my house. I've been leaving messages for her all afternoon, saying I want to talk, but not telling her why. She hates it when I do that but I don't like leaving voicemails, especially about complicated stuff like this; I feel like such a rambling idiot. When I tell her what Rufus told me, she grips my shoulders and jumps up and down with excitement, forcing me to jump too. She's far more thrilled about the fact that Max fancies me than I am, which probably isn't a good sign.

'I thought he liked you!' she practically screams. 'It was so obvious, the way he kept staring at you when you were talking.'

'Was it? Did he?'

'Yeah. Like, derr.' She giggles. 'And what's even better is

that Rufus Justice gave you the news – how cool is that! Just think, if you go out with Max you'll be practically in the Justice family! You'll be a rock star's little sister. Almost.'

'Yeah, but . . .'

She isn't listening. '*Rosie and Max sitting in a tree, k-i-s-s-i-n-g*,' she chants, teasing me.

Oh God, I think, if I go out with him I'll have to kiss him. I picture his face. I can't imagine doing that. That's not a good sign either. I tell her my fears and she tries to reassure me.

'I wasn't into Rich as much as I am now, at first,' she says. 'He was much more into me.' She looks a bit wistful. We both know that now it's the other way around.

'You know what?' she says. 'I think you should go for it. Go out with him one evening, sort of on a date, but not an actual proper date, and see how you feel then. It would be like trying before you buy.'

'Yeah, that's a good idea.'

'It would be so cool if you had a boyfriend too, one who I get on with. Hey, if it works out, you and Max and me and Rich can double date.'

'Yeah, but what about Vix?'

'She'll be OK. She'll get used to the idea. And I'm sure Max has some nice mates he can introduce her to, someone else she'll like. Then all six of us can hang out. Just talk to her, Rosie. Sort it out before she gets upset.'

'I will,' I say. And I do mean to. I know I should call Vix

right now, but I'm too much of a coward. It can't do any harm to leave it a few days, until I have a better idea of how I feel about Max, can it? There's no point upsetting her until I'm sure.

Chapter 11

Testing the Water

It's Friday evening, and tonight is my 'sort of', 'kind of', 'try before you buy' tester date with Max. Max doesn't know this, of course. He thinks it's a real date, a proper first date, and he's made a big effort tonight. He's wearing really smart, dark blue jeans with an actual shirt, which it looks like he's tried to iron, and he's doused himself in too much of Rufus's aftershave again. I think he might even have had his hair cut, although he's still got so much of it, it's hard to tell. I'm slightly more low key, in a hoodie, vintage jeans and Converse. Well, I don't want to look like I've tried too hard and give him the wrong impression, do I? Or maybe I do? I guess that's why I'm here: to find out!

Over the past few days, since he asked if I'd like to go out for dinner tonight, just the two of us, I have tried to make it clear that I'm not sure if I want to be more than friends. I avoid too much eye contact and I'm trying not to play with my hair while we're talking, as I've read this is a sure-fire sign that you like someone. But I don't think he's quite got it. I'm pretty sure Rufus told him what I said, but I also think he might have said I was 'playing hard to get' and, that, unfortunately, has just made Max even keener. He's started looking really intensely into my eyes whenever he talks to me, and when I act shy and uncomfortable, I think he thinks I'm being coy and flirtatious.

I've finally spoken to Vix about what's going on. I knew I had to tell her, but it never seemed to be the right time, so I kept putting it off. I know it's awful, but I left it until the last possible moment. I was hoping Sky might say something for me, but she said that wasn't fair, it was up to me. She also said Vix had been talking about Max a lot, wondering when we're all going to go out again, and that not being honest with her was cruel.

I called her a couple of hours ago. I keep replaying the conversation in my mind.

'Hey, Vix, I need to talk to you about Max,' I began.

'Yes?' She sounded excited. Bum, I knew that was the wrong way to start.

'God, I don't know how to say this. Ur, I might like him too. Maybe. Sort of.'

'But you said you didn't. When I asked you, at the picnic.'

'I know, I'm sorry. I wasn't sure, I was confused . . . I'm still confused. The thing is, God, um, it turns out he likes me. He told Rufus.'

'Oh,' she sounded hurt.

'I'm really sorry, Vix. I know that you've got a bit of a thing for him and all. I didn't mean it to happen and I didn't do anything to make it happen, honest. I was actually going to say something to him about you liking him, before Rufus told me.'

'It's not your fault,' she said, generously. 'It's just the way it goes.'

'Yeah. Thanks, Vix. I knew you'd understand.'

'So how are you going to tell him you're not really interested? Are you going to let him down gently?'

'Um, well, not exactly. Not yet. You know I said I wasn't sure how I feel? Well, I've decided there's only one way to find out. I'm going out with him, like on a date. Er, tonight.'

'What, you're actually going on a date with him?'

'Just to see how I really feel, yes. It won't be that different from the other times I've been out with him. Date's just a label, doesn't mean anything.'

She paused and took a deep breath. 'Rosie, I've known you for ever, and I know you wouldn't go on a date with someone if you didn't think you fancied them. I think you're just doing it for the VIP passes, so you can hang out with Rufus and his mates. You don't really like Max. You've never once said you thought he was cute. If it was anyone else, you wouldn't be going. You'd just have said no. You're becoming totally obsessed with celebrities. It's like you've forgotten about real people.'

'That's not fair,' I said. What she suggested hurt me, because I'm not using Max – although I can't pretend that the thought of backstage passes and a summer with the Fieldstar crew isn't a tiny part of it all. 'I do like Max a lot. You know I do. And we get on so well, I need to see if there's something more there.'

'You said you're going tonight?' She sounded tearful. 'And you never said anything to me till now.'

'I know, I'm so sorry. I didn't want to upset you.'

'Well, you have.'

'I know. And I'm really sorry.'

'Enjoy your date,' she said, and she sounded bitter.

'Thanks.' I tried to think of a way to make things better. 'I promise I'll come round tomorrow and we can catch up properly. I don't like leaving things like this.'

'If you want,' she said.

'So what are you doing tonight?'

'I dunno. Sky's seeing Rich. Some of the girls from school are going to the cinema. Maybe I'll tag along.'

'Cool,' I said. 'Have a good night. Speak tomorrow.'

'Sure.' She didn't say, 'Have a good night too.' She just said, 'I guess you'll tell me all about it tomorrow then, won't you?'

I made a right mess of that, didn't I? I didn't feel good

when I hung up the phone. Vix and I used to do everything together, share everything together. This is one thing we can't share. It feels weird.

So here I am, sitting in a local restaurant, across the table from Max, who can't stop grinning at me. We've come to Marine Ices, which is probably the oldest and best Italian ice cream parlour in London. It's right on my doorstep, just opposite Chalk Farm Station and it serves real, home-made Italian ice cream, in every flavour you can imagine, with tons of sprinkles and sauces. You can take them away in big, fancy cones, or eat them in, in bowls or glasses – knickerbocker glories and all sorts, with wafers sticking out . . . But I'm getting ahead of myself. It isn't dessert time yet. There's also a proper Italian restaurant attached to Marine Ices and that's where we are. The walls are decorated with signed photos of all the celebrities who have been here over the years, actors and musicians and even Hollywood film stars from way back. I gaze at them, trying to figure out who I recognise, and I wonder whether I should ask Max if Rufus has come here yet.

Max is such a gentleman. When we arrived, he held open the door for me and he pulled out my chair behind me (which was a bit unfortunate because I wasn't expecting it). He's asked me what I want to drink and eat, ordered the food for both of us, then waited for me to start when his meal came first. I think he's the sort of guy who'd do this even if you weren't on a date with him. I'm not used to it. It's actually quite lovely.

I'm eating spaghetti pomodoro, which is possibly the least romantic thing you could eat, as the tomato sauce flies everywhere when you slurp the spaghetti. I didn't pick it deliberately to put him off me, honestly. If I'd wanted to do that, I could have had garlic bread, and I didn't. It's just the least calorific thing on the menu, and I'm saving myself for dessert. Max is having a pizza with spicy pepperoni on it. It's the size of a satellite dish, but he's working his way through it impressively. As usual, talking to him is a breeze, even though I'm feeling a bit more self-conscious than I normally do. We talk about our friends, moan about our parents and our teachers. He tells me about the term he decided to turn vegetarian, mainly because he really liked a girl in his class who was an animal rights activist. The problem was, he couldn't resist the lure of a bacon sandwich, and when she found out, their relationship was toast.

He stops talking for a second, and laughs. 'Hey, you've got sauce on your chin.'

'Oh, whoops!'

'Come here, you . . .'

Oh no, he's picked up his napkin and now he's leaning over and, before I can stop him, he's wiping my chin for me.

'You're just like a baby,' he teases. 'So cute.'

No! No! No!

'I'm just super-messy, clumsy, a real klutz. You can't take me anywhere.'

'No, you're all right.' He laughs. 'I'll just buy you a bib for next time.'

I cringe – invisibly, I hope. I still don't know if I want there to be a next time.

All evening, I've been compiling a list in my mind, a chart of pros and cons for going out with Max. So far what I've come up with is this:

Pros:
– He's so chivalrous.
– OK, so he's not my usual type, but he's kind of cute. He has nice eyes and full, soft-looking lips.
– We have so much fun together and I can talk about stuff with him. He's probably the best guy friend I've ever had.
– He is Rufus Justice's brother, etc, etc.

Cons:
– When he's talking and he looks into my eyes and I have to do the same back, because looking away would be rude, instead of feeling all gooey, I find myself wondering if he's got better eyelashes than mine, and if that's a bit of sleep I can see there, in the corner.
– He's not my type. I prefer blue eyes, and his are brown. And his mouth is too big for a boy, almost girlish.
– I'm not sure I really want a boyfriend right now.
– Going out with him would make things difficult with Vix. It already has.

Poor Max has no idea that by the end of the night he might have failed an exam he doesn't know he's taking. Right now, he looks really excited because the waiter has just brought the dessert menus, and his eyes are as big and round as the scoops of ice cream he's about to savour. He can't decide what he wants, so he plumps for four different flavours, topped with chocolate sprinkles and strawberry sauce. I've tried everything on the menu before – I've been here so many times – so I just have a scoop of Belgian chocolate and, even though it doesn't really go, some melon sorbet on the side. It's so fruity I'm sure it must count as one of my five a day. Mum would be proud.

'Wow,' says Max, several times. And, 'Mmm.'

But it soon becomes clear that, despite an impressive effort, he can't finish his ice cream. In fact, he's beginning to look distinctly queasy.

'Want to help me polish it off?' he says, eventually. He holds out his spoon to me, expectantly. I think he actually wants to feed it to me himself.

'Oh, no, I couldn't,' I say. 'Too much pasta.' And it doesn't look that appetising to be honest. All the flavours have melted together with the sauce and sprinkles into a big, soupy mess. 'You finish it. It looks so great, you shouldn't waste a drop.'

If there's one thing I know about boys, it's that they don't ever like to be defeated, even by food. Max plunges his spoon back into his bowl and shovels some more of the gloop into his mouth. 'Mmm,' he says, unconvincingly. 'Mmmm. Mmmm.' A few moments later, he puts down his spoon and groans. 'I can't. I think I feel a bit sick now.'

This could be good news. Obviously, I don't want him to feel ill. But, hopefully, it means he won't feel up to trying to kiss me goodnight. I don't think I'm ready for that.

'Do you want a coffee?' he asks. 'I don't think I can eat or drink another thing.'

'Nah, me neither.'

He asks for the bill and I insist on paying half, even though he says I really don't have to, as it's his treat. But it wouldn't be right to let him.

'How about a walk on Primrose Hill? I'm sure I'll feel better if I have some fresh air.'

'Um . . .' I'm not stupid. I know that going for a stroll on Primrose Hill at night (even though it's still light) equals a romantic walk for two. Unless you're taking your dog, that is. 'I don't know. I think it's a bit late.'

He looks at his watch. 'It's only eight-thirty!'

'I said I'd be home by nine.' This is a lie. What I actually said was, 'See you later.'

'Well, you can text your parents. I'm sure they won't mind if you're half an hour late.'

'No, really, I'm a bit tired. I think we should head back. Sorry.'

'That's OK,' he says. 'Next time.'

He loops his arm through mine, which is fine because I do that with all my friends, and we set off on our walk home. Neither of us talks much: me because I'm deep in thought, him because, I guess, he's still feeling sick.

We stop outside my front door. 'Thank you so much,' he says, dropping my arm and turning to face me. 'I've had such a fab evening.'

'Me too,' I say. I'm not lying. It hasn't been as weird as I thought it might be. 'Thank you.'

He puts his hands on my shoulders and leans in towards me. My stomach tightens and I now know with one hundred per cent certainty that I don't want him to kiss me. I offer him my cheek, instead, and he plants a slightly wet smacker on it.

'Goodnight, Rosie,' he says, smiling. I'm relieved. Maybe he's too much of a gentleman to expect a proper kiss on the first date. 'I'll call you tomorrow.'

I watch him walk away and let himself into Rufus's house. Before I go inside my own house, I stand on the doorstep and look out at my street. Dusk is settling now, but the street lights have not yet come on. Out of the corner of my eye, I think I can see Vix, peeking through a crack in her bedroom curtains. I turn to look properly but, if she was ever there, she's gone.

Chapter 12

Missing Vix

When I say I've known Vix for ever, I mean *for ever*. She moved into the street when I was two, so I can't remember a time when we weren't friends. We went to nursery together, to Brownies, to primary school, and then secondary school. We hung out at the same youth club. We had so much fun. Our families went on holiday together. We even started our periods in the same week. I wouldn't ever want to have to choose between Vix and Sky – they're both my absolute best friends – but if you stuck a gun in my face (which has been known to happen in Camden's edgier streets, although probably not for this reason) and said you'd kill me unless I picked just one of them, I'd pick Vix. Just because.

That's why it hurts so much that she's off with me.

Unlike Sky, who's on the phone at ten a.m. sharp, digging for details, Vix doesn't call me to find out about the date. That isn't surprising, really. If it went well, she won't want to know. If it didn't, she'll feel smug and think it was my own fault – although she'd be too sweet to say it. The problem is, I can't win: if I don't call her and tell her all about it, she'll be upset too, because then she'll think I'm avoiding her.

So, I pick up the phone and call. She lets it ring longer than she usually does, although she might just be in the loo.

'Hey,' she says. 'So you're back then.'

It's a weird thing to say. The date was last night. Did she think I was going to sleep at Marine Ices?

'Yeah, course. How are you? How was your evening?'

'Fine,' she says. 'I stayed in. Didn't *feel* like going out in the end.'

I know this is a dig at me, but I don't rise to it. 'Oh right.' There's a silence. 'I just rang to say hi, really.'

'So how did it go then?'

'OK, fine, well. It was nice.'

'And?'

'And I like him, I really do. But . . .' I hesitate, wondering whether I should say this to her. 'I'm still not sure if I fancy him. I think I might just need to go out with him one more time to make my mind up.'

'Trust me,' she says. 'You don't.'

'I don't need to go out with him one more time to know?'

'No, you don't fancy him.'

Ouch. If I were a bitchy person, which I'm not – at least I hope I'm not – I could say something along the lines of: 'You've never had a boyfriend so how would you even know?' But I don't. Instead, I say, 'You really can't say that, Vix.'

'Why? It's pretty obvious. And I don't like that you're messing him around. It's not fair.'

'I'm not lying to him.'

'Nah, just to yourself.'

I was hoping she might have thawed a bit. Instead, she seems even more annoyed with me. 'I think we should talk about this later,' I say. 'Face to face.'

'If you want. Come over. But I'm not going to say anything different.' She hangs up. I stare at the phone for a minute or so, wondering if I should call her back. I feel sad and empty.

Of course we've fallen out before, briefly, over stupid things. I remember the time when we were twelve and we saw this jacket in Miss Selfridge at exactly the same moment – in the days before we bought most of our clothes at the market – and we both fell in love with it. It came in two colourways: blue and black, and red and black. Neither of us could afford it.

The following week, it was my birthday, so I asked Mum and Dad if I could have it for a present – the red and black one. I was so pleased with that jacket, I wore it home from the shop. Then, a few days later, without warning, Vix bought it too, in the blue and black. She didn't seem to think it was a problem.

'It's not the same,' she said. 'Mine is blue and yours is red. It's not a big deal.'

But I thought we looked so stupid, going out together in our matching jackets, that, even though I adored mine, I ended up putting it to the back of the wardrobe. Vix always claimed she had a right to buy it because she saw it first but, if she did, it was by milliseconds. We didn't talk for three days.

But we've never fallen out over a boy. I don't want her to stop talking to me again, especially as I know this is something far more serious and important than a stupid jacket.

My phone is ringing. It's Max. I take a deep breath before I pick up. I've been thinking all morning what I should say to him if he calls. I still haven't decided. I was hoping he'd call later. To be honest, I was hoping he'd message me. Or better still, text.

He sounds a bit nervous. 'Hey, Rosie, how are you? I had a great night.'

'Good, thanks. Me too. How are you?'

'I'm super,' he says. 'Listen, I know it's short notice, but do you want to come round here for dinner? Tonight?

Rufus asked me to ask you.'

'Tonight?'

'Yeah. There's going to be six other people. Jon, the bassist from Fieldstar, and his girlfriend, Anna, Rob, the lead singer and his girlfriend, Julie, and Simon, the lead guitarist, with Karen. Oh, plus Rufus and Isabella, of course.'

'Cool,' I say, trying not to betray just how excited I am. Dinner at Rufus's was fantastic enough, but this is a Proper. Celebrity. Dinner. I have a vague recollection that I'm supposed to be meeting up with Sky and Vix tonight, some clothes-swapping thing arranged yonks ago, but they'll understand. It's not every day you get to have dinner with the whole of Fieldstar! I'm going to meet them all at last! And how brilliant that Rufus wants me to come round *again*. I wonder what Isabella will cook this time? Ooh, I hope she does those melting chocolate puddings for dessert . . .

And then it hits me. Everybody there, except for me and Max, will be in a couple. I think he thinks I'm his girlfriend now. I think *Rufus* thinks I'm Max's girlfriend now. How to put this? 'Er, all couples?'

'Yeah, that's OK, isn't it?'

Is he asking me if I'm OK with being a couple, or just if I don't mind that the others are?

'I guess so,' I say, but I'm not sure which question I'm answering.

'It'll be like a quadruple date kind of thing. Obviously,

I'd rather go out with you alone for our second date but Rufus really wants you to come. We can go out on our own another time.'

'Sure, why not?'

Maybe it's not so bad. I was planning on a second tester date soon, wasn't I? And, this way, I won't have to be alone with Max if I finally decide I'm not interested. Maybe being around the whole of Fieldstar will rub off on him and he'll suddenly seem super attractive to me. It could be just what we need to kickstart things.

When I check the notes on my phone, it turns out I *am* supposed to be going to a clothes-swapping evening tonight at Sky's, with Vix and a few friends from school. I ring Sky, to tell her the bad news. She says she totally understands, she wishes she could come to the Fieldstar dinner too (I think she's angling for an invite, but it's not mine to give) and she'll forgive me, as long as I promise to get her every member of Fieldstar's autograph.

Then I go round to see Vix, like I said I would. We have an awkward, stilted conversation, and I know I need to sort things out with her properly when there's more time. I'm just not sure how. At least she's still talking to me. When I tell her I can't make tonight, she shrugs, like she's disappointed but not surprised. I swear I will make it up to her. We'll have a girly night, just the two of us, doing something fun. Soon.

Chapter 13

Dinner With Fieldstar

I dress up for the evening – not for Max, but for Rufus and his band mates. I'm wearing my newest, coolest, slinkiest dress. I bought it in the market (of course) and it's vintage Eighties, some Japanese designer. The stallholder said it would be worth a packet in a few years, if I looked after it. I don't really care about that. I'm just glad it fits well and that the colour (a lovely shade of purple) suits me.

Max offers to come round and pick me up, so we can arrive together like the others, but I tell him he doesn't need to – I'm only next door! I get there at seven-thirty prompt, heaps earlier than anyone else, which isn't exactly the 'red carpet' entrance I was hoping for. I sit and chat to

Max, and we play a bowling game on Rufus's Wii. Max beats me every time. To be fair, he's probably had loads of practice. It seems that rock stars aren't that hot on punctuality, or maybe they just don't wear watches. They all roll in together, with Rufus (they've been having pre-dinner drinks at the local wine bar), at nine o'clock.

There's a lot of noise from the hall when the others arrive. Nervously, I jump up from the sofa, smooth down my dress and try to look sophisticated. I watch as the members of Fieldstar file into the room, one by one, my wall poster brought to life. First, comes Rufus. He kisses me on the cheek and punches Max on the shoulder. Then there's Jon, who's shorter than the others, and shyer. I know this because it said so in a magazine interview. It also said his favourite food is chocolate and his favourite colour is green. He nods at me, shyly. Simon, who's thin and wiry (favourite food: beans on toast; favourite colour: blue), grins. Finally, there's Rob, who is tall and dark and gorgeous (always refuses to answer stupid questions in magazine interviews). He doesn't seem to notice me at all. I can hear their girlfriends in the hall, talking to Isabella. I wonder if this is where I'm supposed to be too.

'Rosie, meet Simon, Jon and Rob,' says Rufus. 'Guys, this is my little brother's girlfriend, Rosie. She lives next door. Her dad's the one designing our new album cover.'

I open my mouth to say something about not really being Max's girlfriend, then shut it again. This isn't the time. I glance at Max. He looks happy. So I smile, and shake everybody's hand, and think that if, two months ago, someone had told me I'd soon be standing in the house next door, shaking hands with the whole of Fieldstar, I'd have had them shipped off to the nearest mental asylum. Two months ago, I would also have said that meeting Fieldstar might just be the most exciting thing that could ever happen to me. It isn't. It feels . . . normal.

The girls come in. They're all pretty, in an understated way. They're all wearing jeans. I fold my arms protectively over my dress and smile, as if I don't have a care in the world. They peer at me and smile back. It's a bit like being next to the clique of cool girls at school and knowing that, however friendly they seem, you'll never be one of them. Isabella does the introductions this time, then heads back into the kitchen.

Max and I have to squash up close on the sofa because there isn't really enough room in here for everyone. We're so close that I can feel his pulse. His heart is beating very fast. Oh God, now I think his arm is creeping around the back of the chair, sort of around me, but it could just be the most comfortable way for him to sit. I look straight ahead, in case he's trying to stare into my eyes again. And then, because I feel so awkward, I do something deeply out of character.

I say: 'I should go and see if Isabella needs some help.'

Mum would be so proud. For the few seconds before she dropped dead of a heart attack, anyway.

I clamber up, trying not to knock into Max, and go into the kitchen. Isabella is juggling pans at an impressive cooker. It's a mint green colour and it takes up half the room. I stare at it, open-mouthed, like it's some kind of Tardis.

'Hello, Rosie. You like Argarr? She eez my baby,' purrs Isabella.

Isabella has a baby? Does Rufus know? 'Sorry? Who's Argarr?'

She strokes the green monster. 'Aga. Zee cooker. You like?'

I have met people who call their dogs and cats their babies. One of my friends at school loves her iPhone so much that she jokes it's her baby. But a cooker? 'Oh yes, it's, er, she's lovely. What are you making? Can I do anything?'

'Most eez fineeshed. You can help make a hollandaise, no?'

I have no idea what a hollandaise is, but I have a feeling it probably doesn't contain windmills or clogs. 'I'm sorry, Isabella. I can't cook. Tell me what to do and I'll try.'

'Your mama no teach you?'

'No. She can't cook either.'

She looks shocked. 'What she do?'

'She's a doctor. At the local health centre.'

'Ah, yes. I go there. Rufus too. But what you eat at home?'

'You don't want to know,' I say. 'Ready meals mostly. With tons of salad and fruit.'

'I teach you,' she says, smiling.

It turns out hollandaise is a sort of bright yellow mayonnaise that's made out of egg yolks and butter. We're having it with asparagus as a starter. I'm not sure I like asparagus, and Dad says it makes your pee smell funny. But at least I'm learning something very useful. I now know not only how to make a cup of tea, boil an egg and make a microwave meal – to date, the sum total of my cooking skills – I'll also be able to rustle up a mean hollandaise. I wonder if it goes with cheese and onion crisps.

Isabella doesn't seem to mind that I'm watching, rather than doing. She's amazing: beautiful, clever and a brilliant cook. I'm only ever going to be close to being one of those things (clue, not the first, or the last), and that's debatable. That's why I'm probably never going to date a rock star.

'Eez good that you and Max are together now, no?' she says, as she stirs furiously.

I blush. 'Sort of. We're not really together. I mean, it's early days.'

'He eez nice boy, no? Kind boy. You should snap heem up. If my leetle sister eez in London, I introduce her.'

I feel a pang of jealousy, which surprises me. I'm not sure I want Max, but I'm darn sure I don't want Isabella's little sister – no doubt beautiful, clever and the winner of the Czech version of *Junior Masterchef* – to have him. 'Is she coming to stay?' I ask, nervously.

'No, she need veeza. Not have.'

'Shame,' I say.

Isabella says she's got things under control, so I go back into the living room. Max grins at me and I feel a little burst of affection for him. I sit down next to him and when his leg brushes against mine, I don't move away. The others are chatting loudly, laughing and joking about things they've done and people I don't know. It's hard to join in with the conversation because everyone knows each other so well. Instead, I smile and nod a lot, and hope dinner will be soon. I've hardly eaten anything today and I'm starving.

Finally, Isabella comes into the room and announces that dinner is ready. She says that as it's such a lovely, warm night, we should eat outside. I also suspect the dinner table isn't big enough for all ten of us. I've never been in Rufus's garden before – although I've tried to peek over the wall a few times – and it's beautiful. There are Moroccan jewelled lanterns and giant candles everywhere and huge, multicoloured cushions spread out around a low, ancient wooden table. In one corner, there's a little alcove, covered by swathes of transparent fabric in rich colours. I want to say, 'Wow!' but no one else looks that impressed. I guess they've seen it before.

Isabella tells everyone to sit down on the cushions and then she brings out the food. First comes the starter, with the hollandaise I couldn't make. I put a huge dollop on my asparagus. I don't really like it, but maybe it will stop my pee from smelling. Then there's some sort of spicy chicken dish, with rice and salad and, for dessert, an amazing passion fruit cheesecake, with exotic fruit salad. I wonder if Isabella would give Mum cooking lessons. Not that Mum would have time.

It's weird to see Rufus with his band mates. He doesn't seem so important, somehow, or so sure of himself, or even so charismatic or good-looking. I'm learning that there's a definite pecking order in bands, and even though Fieldstar call themselves a 'democracy' (which means they all write the songs together and share the money), the drummer comes right at the bottom. Everyone is talking about a film about an old band called Spinal Tap, which I've never seen, but which is supposed to be hilarious. And particularly funny about drummers. In the film, all the drummers have really bad luck. They die in crazy ways, like spontaneously combusting on stage, or being killed in bizarre gardening accidents. I must ask Dad to rent the DVD. Max says it's a fifteen, so it's touch and go whether Mum will let me watch it. I might get away with it, as I am very nearly fifteen. Rufus says I should point out it's a documentary, so it is clearly educational. Everybody laughs at this; I don't get the joke, but I pretend to.

'It's a spoof,' Max whispers to me, kindly. 'Not really a documentary.'

'Course,' I say. 'I knew that.'

'Hey, what's the difference between a drummer and a drum machine?' says Simon. He pauses, and Rob and Jon shout in unison, 'You only have to punch the information into the machine once!'

Everyone laughs really hard, even Rufus. I can tell he doesn't think it's that funny though.

'What do you call someone who hangs around with musicians?' says Rob. 'A drummer!'

Simon again: 'What do you call a drummer who's just split up with his girlfriend? Homeless.'

Rufus groans and, not very chivalrously, tries to deflect the jokes on to me. 'Very funny, guys. Do you know what Rosie's surname is? Buttery. Buttery, I tell you!'

'Lovely name,' says Rob. 'You should be ashamed of yourself, Rufus, picking on teenage girls. Anyway, how do you know it's the drummer at the door?'

'He doesn't know when to come in,' sing-songs Simon. 'Boom boom.'

'Let's change the subject,' says Karen. She's the sweetest of the girlfriends, not counting Isabella, and the only one who has tried to talk to me properly. Earlier, she told me she likes my dress, and asked me where I got it from. 'So, Rosie, how long have you and Max been seeing each other?'

On second thoughts, I think I'd rather talk about drummers. 'Um, er, I . . .'

'About a day,' says Max. 'We had our first proper date last night. But we've been friends for a while.' He beams at me.

'Aren't they sweet?' says Rufus. He hugs Isabella. Karen nods, and takes Simon's hand. Max takes mine. I let him. It feels OK, not horrible, not wonderful, not even weird. Just OK.

So that's it. In the end, other people have decided for me: I am now Max's girlfriend. We are going out. We are an official couple. An item. I'm still not convinced that I want to be, but I'm going to give it a go. Mum has always said I give up on things too easily, that I should make more of an effort. This time, I'm going to do just that.

Chapter 14

My Accidental Boyfriend

Last night, Sky went out with a jacket she didn't wear any more and came home with two new tops. I went out single and came home with a boyfriend.

'Oh my God!' she squeals, when I call her to fill her in. 'I'm so excited! So what happened?'

'That's the thing,' I say. 'Nothing happened. We ate dinner, talked with the others, and that was it. Everyone automatically thought Max was my boyfriend – including Max – so I just decided to go with the flow.'

'Oh, I see,' she says, though it doesn't sound like she does. 'I guess that's good. I didn't want to say anything, but all your um-ing and ah-ing was getting a teensy bit boring. For everyone. So . . . did you kiss him?'

'God, no,' I say. 'Just a friendly peck on the cheek, when I left. I was the first one to go – as usual, thanks, Mum – and I gave everyone a quick kiss goodbye, Max included. We were all still in the garden. I was hardly going to have my first snog with Max in front of the whole of Fieldstar, was I?'

She ponders this. 'I'm sure tons of people snog in front of them at their gigs. They're used to it.'

'It's not the same thing, and you know it!'

'Hmm.' She and Rich can't keep their hands off each other, so she's probably finding this difficult to understand. 'Anyway, did you get their autographs for me?'

'Er, no, sorry.'

'Oh Rosie, I knew you'd forget.'

'I didn't forget, exactly.' I say, although the truth is, I did, until it was practically time to leave, and then I couldn't bring myself to ask. 'It just seemed a bit weird. You know, pass the salt and, by the way, could you sign your autograph for my friend Sky?'

'Fair enough, I guess. But now you're Max's *girlfriend*, I'm sure you can get them for me sometime. As well as all the insider gossip.'

'OK,' I say. 'I'll ask Max to ask Rufus to ask them for you.'

'Cool. So have you talked to Vix yet?'

I sigh. 'Not today. But she's barely speaking to me. It's horrible.'

'I know,' she says. 'She mentioned it last night. She's not so much upset about Max, she's hurt about the way you told her. Or didn't tell her for so long. And she's mad you dropped us all last night to go to Rufus's. She thinks you're being really shallow.'

That hurts, even though I already know what Vix thinks. For some reason, hearing it from Sky makes it feel worse. 'I'm not,' I say. 'Honestly. You know that, yeah? I wouldn't normally do that – it was just an amazing opportunity. And as for not telling her, I was just trying not to upset her. Now I've got to tell her we're actually going out, it's gonna be even worse.'

'Hmm, glad I'm not you,' Sky says, unhelpfully.

'Cheers, Sky!'

'Sorry,' she says. 'But what can I do? I'll stick up for you as much as I can, but in the end it's between you and her, isn't it?'

'Yeah. . .'

'And I'm off to India next week, remember, so I won't be around to help.'

Sky's mum is taking her whole family to a yoga retreat in Goa for a month. Sky doesn't want to go. She says it will be all meditation sessions at five a.m. with nasty smells, weird noises and hideous food. She asked if she could stay with me instead, and my parents were OK with it, but her mum put her foot down and said she had to go. Apparently, it will be good for her spiritual growth, whatever that means. Sky says it will serve her mum right if she runs off with a gap-year hippy. On an elephant.

'Bummer.'

'Yup. So when are you seeing Max again?'

'I dunno. I guess he'll call me.'

'Ooh, stop it, Rosie, I can't take your enthusiasm! You're, like, soooo excited!'

'Don't be sarcastic. I just need to get used to the idea.'

'He's a hot guy, Rosie. It shouldn't be that hard.'

'I know. I'm getting there.'

'OK. But I probably won't buy a hat yet. Or a turban, in Goa.'

'Eh?'

'For your wedding.'

'No,' I say. 'Please don't do that. Anyway, I don't think Fieldstar play weddings. And I'm not planning to get married until I'm at least thirty-five.'

I see an image of myself walking down an aisle somewhere, wearing a vintage beaded wedding dress that, naturally, I picked up in the market. Rufus is the best man, Amy Winehouse organised my hen night, and the paparazzi flashes are popping so manically they're blinding me. 'Rosie Justice' has a nice ring to it, I think. The only problem is that I can't ever imagine wanting to marry Max. Not unless I could just shake his hand after the vow part.

Vix isn't around when I call her, so I leave a message asking her to ring me back. I've told Sky not to say anything; I don't want Vix to think she's the last to know again. Then I decide to call Max. I should show willing, right? As the phone rings, I repeat the words 'Max is my boyfriend' out loud, to try to drill the idea into my brain. Sky's mum calls that a mantra. Apparently, if you say a phrase enough times, you can make anything seem normal.

'Max is my boyfriend. Max is my boyfriend. Max is my boyfriend. Max is my boyfriend. Max is my boyfriend. Max is my boyfriend. Max is my . . .'

Max is picking up the phone. 'Hellloooo,' he says, sounding incredibly pleased to hear from me. 'How are you? Wasn't last night great?'

'Yeah,' I say. 'It was. I had a brilliant time.'

'Great! The Fieldstar crew all really liked you,' he says. 'You fitted right in.'

'Really?' I am beaming. 'That's amazing.'

'Yeah. So, they said, if you want to be my "plus one" at any of the after-show parties at the gigs this summer, starting with the G Festival in a few of weeks, you're in.'

'Fantastic.' Oh my God! 'Definitely.'

I haven't asked Mum and Dad if I can go to the G Festival yet, but I'll worry about that later.

'Listen,' he says, taking a deep breath. 'I hope you weren't embarrassed about the boyfriend/girlfriend thing. They just sort of assumed.'

'Er, yeah.' I feel my face flush, and I'm glad he can't see.

'So we're all right, then?'

'Sure we are.'

'And we are, er, boyfriend and girlfriend? Going out?'

'Uh, yeah, I guess we are. If that's what you want to call it.' Oh dear, that doesn't sound very enthusiastic. Maybe I should make out I'm just being cool. 'Who needs labels?' I add.

'Great. So, I was wondering, do you want to meet up tonight, have our proper second date? The cinema, maybe?'

I hesitate. It feels too soon for me. And I really do need to sort things out with Vix. 'I'm sorry, Max. I can't. It's not that I don't want to, but I should see Vix tonight. I kind of bailed out of something I was supposed to be doing with her last night, and she's a bit upset.'

'Oh, right, of course.' He sounds disappointed.

'Tomorrow would be good, though.'

He brightens. 'OK, tomorrow it is.'

By the evening, Vix still hasn't returned my calls, so I decide to turn up at her house unannounced. I feel weirdly nervous about going, even though I must have been round a million times in my life. I take round one of the dresses I might have donated to last night's clothes swap. It's a shift dress from the Sixties, with a green paisley pattern on it. Vix has always admired it and, now that she's lost a little bit of weight, it should fit her perfectly. It's my peace offering. Instead of swapping it for her clothes, I'm swapping it for her forgiveness.

But Vix isn't in. When her mum opens the door she looks surprised to see me.

'Oh, sorry, Rosie, but Vicky's not here. She's gone out with one of your friends from school. Katy, I think. Anyway, you should be able to get her on her mobile.'

'Right,' I say. I shuffle from foot to foot on the doorstep, unsure what to say or do. 'I'll, er, call her then.' I don't want Vix's mum to know I've already tried, and Vix isn't returning my calls.

Maybe she's guessed. Or maybe Vix has said something about falling out with me, because her mum looks at me with a kindly, sympathetic expression. 'I'll tell her you came round if you like. Get her to call you when she comes in.'

'Thanks. And will you give her this from me?' I hand over the plastic bag containing the dress. 'It's a sort of gift.'

Vix's mum smiles. 'Of course,' she says. 'Take care of yourself, Rosie, and see you soon.' She moves to close the front door.

'Actually,' I say, holding out my hand to stop her, 'maybe I should leave a note with it.' I fish in my bag for a bit of paper and a pen and then, in my neatest scrawl write:

To Vix,

A pressie for you to say sorry for everything.

Call me!

Best friends, always,

R xxxxx

I fold it over twice and hand it to Vix's mum, who drops it inside the carrier bag with the dress. It's only later that I realise I've written the note on the back of a napkin from Marine Ices. That could seem a little insensitive. I hope Vix doesn't notice.

Chapter 15

The Anti-Date

o wt film do y want 2 c?

The text is from Max. It's five o'clock in the afternoon and our date is only a couple of hours away. I'm not sure that going to the cinema is such a good idea now. The more I think about it, the more I think that Max only wants to take me there because it's dark inside, and he plans to kiss me. If that weren't the case, he would have suggested seeing a specific film, wouldn't he? Instead, he's leaving the choice up to me, saying he's not bothered what we see, which I guess is code for: *I'm not planning to be looking at the screen very much. Nudge. Nudge.*

Oh God.

I can't blame him for trying, really. Strictly speaking, this is date number three, and all he's had is a peck on the cheek. If it were the other way around, I'd be starting to wonder if he really fancies me. I wonder if he is starting to wonder that. Or if he thinks I'm just taking things super slow.

I study the Camden Odeon listings online. There are five films showing tonight: a romantic comedy, some weird Japanese film with subtitles, an action film about the war in Iraq, a nasty horror with gruesome torture and a cartoon about a giant dog with superpowers. Something for everyone, it seems. But which one is most suitable for me, the girl who doesn't want to be kissed? I read through the list again, and sigh. There's only one film that I actually want to see, the one I'd plump for without question if I were going to the cinema with Sky or Vix tonight. The romantic comedy is based on a book I've read and stars an actress from my favourite American series. It sounds great. But, for obvious reasons, I cannot see anything romantic with Max. It might give him *ideas*.

So it comes down to this: which film is the ultimate turn off? I consider the horror (no one normal wants to snog while people are being tortured, do they), but rule it out instantly. Mainly because I'm a wuss and when I feel scared I tend to reach for the nearest hand – or leap into the nearest lap – which would again give Max completely the wrong message. But scary's out anyway – the film has an eighteen certificate. Which leaves action movie, cartoon or weird foreign film.

The action movie (no one normal wants to snog while people are being blown up, do they?) would have been good, except it's three hours long and I've promised I'll be home early tonight. The cartoon could work. The screening will be full of annoying kids with their mums, who'll disapprove if there's any kissing action going on. But the last showing is at six p.m. So that's out too. Which leaves just one option: weird Japanese film with subtitles it is, then.

Max picks me up at seven-thirty. He seems more nervous than usual, and his palms are really sweaty. I find this out when he grasps my hand as we walk down Camden Road towards Parkway, where the cinema is. I pretend not to notice. But when he drops my hand to press the button on the pedestrian crossing, I ever so discreetly wipe it on my jeans.

'You're full of surprises, Rosie,' he says, as we approach the cinema. 'I had no idea you liked Japanese films.' He sounds pleased with my choice.

'Oh yes,' I say. 'Japanese films are the best. Not that I've seen many, but the ones I have seen are, like, really good. Very . . . er . . . Japanese.' I wrack my brains, trying desperately to think of another Japanese film I've sat through in my lifetime, so I can say something intelligent about it. I can't. The truth is, the only Japanese thing I know anything about is *Hello Kitty.* When I was six, I used to have a *Hello Kitty* pencil case, notebook and bag. I glance up at Max. Should I tell him this? Will he be impressed?

'I'm really into manga,' he says, before I can decide.

'Oh yeah? Great. Me too.' I'm not totally sure what manga is. I'm guessing it's probably like sushi. I don't like sushi.

He grins at me, mischievously. 'Rufus thought you'd definitely want to see the chick flick – the one with the stupid trailer that's on TV all the time. I probably shouldn't tell you this, but he even bet me a tenner you would.' He reaches into his back pocket and pulls out a crisp ten pound note. 'Good thing you didn't,' he says, looking pleased with himself. 'I told him I knew you had better taste than that. He was seriously impressed. We can spend it on sweets and drinks if you want.'

'Thanks,' I say, feeling like a fraud. Funny, I think, that Rufus seems to know me better than Max does.

The weird Japanese film with subtitles turns out to be a weird Japanese romance with subtitles. That'll teach me not to read the small print. And guess what? Japanese snogging isn't all that much different from American or English snogging, it's just that the people doing it are Japanese. Plus, you need to read the words on the screen to understand what they're saying before and after they start making squelching noises. And guess what again?

Even Japanese snogging with subtitles gives Max *ideas*.

Worse, because the film is a bit weird and confusing, and reading the subtitles is hard work, and there's hardly anyone else in that screen, he seems very keen to put these ideas into action very quickly. Fifteen minutes in, and I can feel his arm creeping around the back of my chair and finding its way across my shoulders. He leaves his hand dangling just above my chest, then leans in towards me, resting his head on my shoulder. I drop my popcorn in alarm, scattering half of it across the floor.

'Oops, sorry!' I exclaim. Leaning away from his embrace, I force him to take back his hand so I can bend forward in my seat to retrieve my popcorn. But once I'm sitting up straight again, the popcorn safely balanced on my lap, he tries again. I feel his hand wandering around my back, his fingers brushing across the nape of my neck. I can sense that he has turned his body towards mine, in anticipation that I'll do the same, so I sit dead straight towards the screen, pretending I'm concentrating hard. His hand begins to stroke the back of my hair. It tickles. Then I feel his breath, very close to my ear. It tickles even more, and I want to giggle. At the last second, I duck away from him and he pulls back. Even in the dim light, I can see he looks hurt. Maybe, I think, I should just let him kiss me, and get it over with. He might be a good kisser – I might even enjoy it, despite myself. But I can't do it. It doesn't feel right. I guess I'm still not ready. 'Um, Max, I don't really like PDAs,' I whisper, by way of an apology. 'I get a bit self-conscious in front of other people. Sorry.'

Max nods, as though he understands, but he still looks crestfallen, so I try to make up for it. 'Would you like some popcorn?' I ask, holding out the packet. Not really much consolation, I know. He shakes his head. Feeling guilty, I let him hold my hand for a few minutes, until he gets cramp in his elbow from supporting his arm on the rest in between us.

'Are you enjoying this?' he whispers. 'The film, I mean?'

I turn to him and shake my head. 'Not really.' That's an understatement. I have no clue what's going on.

'Wanna go somewhere else?'

'OK.'

We creep out as quietly as we can, trying not to disturb the other people in our row. Someone tuts. It annoys me because I'm doing my best to be polite, so I tut back. Max laughs at me and grabs my arm to steer me out of the way.

It's still light outside, which is somehow always a surprise when you come out of the cinema. We stop at the entrance and screw up our eyes in discomfort.

'I've got a question for you,' says Max. 'What the hell was that man doing to the tree?'

'God knows.'

'And why were all those girls dressed in sheets running all the time?'

'Honestly? I have no clue.'

'But, Rosie, I thought you said you really wanted to see this film.'

'Um. I thought it was something else,' I say. 'I made a mistake. Sorry.' I pause. 'Do you think Rufus will want his popcorn money back?'

He laughs. 'Nah, you're safe. Anyway, he doesn't need to know. So, want to watch a DVD at mine instead?'

'OK.'

Thankfully, nobody's in when we get home, so I don't have to attempt to discuss Japanese art movies with Rufus. Max leads me into the front room and tells me to make myself comfortable while he sorts out the film.

'There's a whole library of DVDs here,' he says, digging around in a cupboard next to the televison. 'How about *Batman*? Or would you rather watch *Fieldstar on Tour*? *Fieldstar in Concert*? *Fieldstar Live at the Palladium*?'

'*Batman*'s fine,' I say. 'Your choice this time.'

He laughs. 'Probably wise.'

After putting on the DVD, he dims the lights and then he comes and sits down next to me on the sofa. It isn't long before his arm has snaked behind my back and over my shoulders again. We watch the film quietly for a while, and then he takes a long, deep breath. 'I'd really like to kiss you, Rosie,' he says, eventually. 'No one can see us here, I promise. It's totally private.'

I can tell it's taken a lot for him to say it. I feel my cheeks burning. No boy has ever been quite so direct with me before, and I don't know how to respond. My first instinct is to lie. I want to say, 'The thing is, this is really embarrassing, but I'm getting that tingle, the one that says you're about to have a cold sore.' But I don't want to hurt him again. And anyway, he's living next door, so how will I explain it when the cold sore never materialises?

'I know you do, Max. I'm just shy,' I tell him. I am *so* not shy. Vix and Sky would laugh their heads off if they heard that, but they're not here, and, fortunately, Max has never seen how I behave with other boys.

'Ah,' he says, stroking my back. 'Don't be shy. You're so sweet, Rosie.'

'No, I'm not,' I whisper, but I don't think he hears. The irony is, suddenly I really do feel shy. Shy and self-conscious and gawky, like I've never kissed anyone before.

'No pressure. Just give me a kiss on the cheek, then, if you prefer,' he says.

'OK,' I say, relieved.

He leans towards me and points to the centre of his cheek with his finger. I pucker up my lips, ready to plant a kiss on target when, without warning, he turns his face ninety degrees to the right. There's an awkward clash of lips and noses.

'Sorry,' he says, not sounding at all sorry. 'I couldn't help myself. Do it again. I promise this time I'll keep my head perfectly still.'

'OK,' I say, puckering up again. I move my face towards

his, more cautiously this time, ready to pull back if he tries his trick again. I should have known – just as my lips are about to make contact with his cheek, he pulls exactly the same stunt. I duck my face away, but I can't help laughing. 'Max! You're so cheeky!' I cry.

He's laughing too. 'Sorry, I promise I won't do that again. You have my word. Maybe.'

'OK. But I don't really believe you.' All this head bobbing is making me dizzy. If he wants to kiss me this much, I think, perhaps I should let him. And so, on my third attempt, when he tries the same sneaky move, I don't duck away from him. I keep my face still and let him press his mouth on to mine. He seems surprised for a second, and then he takes my face in his hands and kisses me properly. He's not a bad kisser. He has soft, full lips and a firm but gentle technique. I feel . . .

I feel . . .

I feel . . . absolutely nothing. Zilch. Zero. Nada. I might as well be chewing a piece of gum that's lost its flavour. The kiss seems to be going on for ever. I had no idea kissing could be so boring. What's that black thing on the wallpaper? Is it a squashed fly? Oh God, what have I started?

'Thank you,' he says, eventually, drawing away. His face is flushed and his eyes have taken on a dreamy, glassy look. 'I've been wanting to do that for so long.' He strokes my hair.

'Me too,' I say, because to say anything else would be cruel.

'You're so beautiful, Rosie,' he says.

'You too,' I say, because my mind has now gone completely blank. 'I mean, thank you.'

I tell him it's time for me to go and he insists on walking me to my garden gate, even though I say it isn't necessary.

'I'm so happy,' he says, kissing me again, when he's sure my parents can't see us through the window. 'See you tomorrow.'

I wave goodbye and let myself into the house, hoping that Mum and Dad won't grill me about the date. I'm surprised to find everyone, including Charlie – who should be in bed – in the living room, watching TV.

'Where's Rosie been?' asks Charlie.

'Rosie's been to the cinema with her new boyfriend,' says Dad, grinning at me. 'They've been on a *date*.'

'Eughhh,' says Charlie, who is at the stage when little boys think that little girls are disgusting. He can't imagine why a boy and a girl would want to talk to each other, let alone kiss.

'Yeah,' I say, under my breath. 'I know how you feel.'

Chapter 16

Kissing Adam Grigson

When I first learned to ride a bike, I was hopeless at it. Dad would take off my stabilisers and I'd manage to cycle for about a metre before I'd tip over to one side or the other and collapse. He'd pick me up, rub my bruises better, put me back on the bike and hold on to me while I tried again. And again. And again. And then one day, he let go and I didn't realise I was cycling on my own until I'd reached the end of the garden. After that, it was plain, er, cycling.

So maybe it's the same with kissing. With some people, it just comes naturally. You move towards them, they move towards you and your mouths fit together like magnets, even if your eyes are closed. With others, it takes practice (but, just to be clear, not my dad's help. Ewww). Perhaps the more I do it with Max, the easier and better it will get until, one day, I'll forget I have to try at all and I'll find myself enjoying it. In the meantime, there are loads of things I can do to make it less of a chore. The night after our first kiss, when Max came round, I closed my eyes and imagined I was kissing Adam Grigson (without the fangs), and it helped a lot. And so that's what I've been doing, for the last week or so, to get through it. The trouble is, it doesn't seem to be working as well, any more.

I wish I could talk about this with Sky, but she's in Goa now, and I guess it's a bit difficult to use your phone while you're sitting in the lotus position, chanting mantras. She's promised to message me as soon as she can find an internet café. I can't talk about it with Vix, obviously, even though we are at least speaking again. She loved the dress and told me I didn't need to give her presents to say sorry and that, of course, we'd always be best friends. But something feels different. There's a great big Max-shaped block in between us. When we talk, we try to talk about everything *except* him, which is crazy, as there's not that much else going on for me right now, and so there are tons of weird silences. And whenever, inevitably, the subject of Max does come up, she sounds like she doesn't really want to hear about what's happening with him. So, I feel like I have to lie to her. I've told her that I've realised I was wrong and that now I'm one hundred per cent sure I really do fancy Max, after all, and that I'm really happy being his girlfriend. Saying it made me feel a bit sick. She hasn't said it outright, but I can tell she's thinking, 'Who are you really trying to convince here?'

I am not going to worry about any of that right now because today it's the G Festival in Regent's Park and I'm on the guest list as Max's 'plus one'. Mum and Dad didn't take much persuading in the end. Once they realised the festival was only up the road, and that I wouldn't be staying in a tent with boys, or getting trench foot, they were perfectly happy to let me come. Max promised them he'd look after me too.

I have no idea what the 'G' in G festival stands for. Nor, it turns out, does anyone else. Max said it's probably 'G' for guitar, or G-string (as in the musical note, not the underwear, I hope), as all the bands playing are guitar bands, like Fieldstar. Isabella said it's 'G' for Green because it's in the park. Rufus laughed and said it must be 'G' for G-spot. I think I've heard of it, but I'm not completely sure what it is. Isabella slapped Rufus, so I thought better of checking.

Being on the guest list means I'm wearing a red wristband which allows me to go in the VIP area, where there are free drinks and snacks and proper seats. It also means that I get to use a proper, clean toilet with soap and towels. Everyone else — the people who've actually paid for their tickets – has a green band, which means they have to queue for hours for smelly portaloos, sit on the grass and buy their own food and drink. It's not really fair, is it? The weird thing is, my red band makes me feel ever so important, like I'm a celebrity too, like I'm better than the people wearing green wristbands. Now I can see why some celebrities start to act so spoiled and full of themselves and start demanding ridiculous backstage riders. I asked Max what Fieldstar have on their rider. It's pretty dull: just some mineral water, fruit and biscuits. But he told me that when Rufus and his band mates first started playing big gigs they'd compete to dream up the most ridiculous demands, just for fun. Once, Rufus asked for a boar's head, three orchids and a pint of fig juice, to be presented on a silver platter by a milkmaid. I think he got a ham sandwich, a cup of tea and a reputation for being a diva in a gossip mag instead.

Fieldstar are headlining, so I've got hours to enjoy the rest of the festival with Max, to hang around in the VIP area, listen to the other bands, or check out the stalls. The atmosphere is incredible. Everybody is walking around with huge grins, like it's Christmas and their birthday and the end of term, all rolled into one. I can't wait till I'm older and I'm allowed to go with my friends to one of the big festivals, like Glastonbury, where people camp out for three whole days and nights. Dad went when he was young and he still tells cringe-making stories about it. I think he'd like us all to go as a family but there is no way on earth I am ever going to a music festival with my parents. Dad would do his embarrassing sing-along-dance thing and Mum would probably go around telling people to stop drinking so much and warning them about skin cancer.

I've just wandered out of the VIP tent, holding hands with Max, when I bump into Lisa, the bitchy girl from school. She greets me like we're best mates, and I find myself telling her that Rufus Justice is my next-door neighbour.

'And,' I nod towards Max, who is right next to me, holding my hand, 'this is my boyfriend, Max – Rufus's brother.'

Max grins and squeezes my hand. I guess it's the first time I've ever called him my boyfriend in public. He looks so proud to be seen with me, with ME, Little Miss Nobody, that I feel guilty for trading on his famous brother's name to introduce him.

Lisa looks him up and down, approvingly. 'I'm Lisa,' she says, holding out her hand. 'A friend of Rosie's from school.'

What a cheek! I don't think she's spoken more than two words to me in the past three years. Oblivious, Max shakes Lisa's hand and smiles his big, friendly grin at her.

'So, anyway, really nice to see you and all, but we've got to go, haven't we, Max?' I say, before Lisa can try to schmooze her way into our group. 'We're meeting Sky over by the jewellery stall, and we're late. Sorry, Lisa.'

Max looks puzzled. 'But I thought Sky was in . . .'

'. . . In her own little world as usual! Come on, we'd better find her before she goes off on her own again.'

'Oh right,' says Lisa, with transparent disappointment. 'Maybe see you later then.'

'Maybe,' I say, giving her my best fake smile. 'Have a nice time.'

As we walk away, I giggle. 'I can't believe her nerve,' I say to Max. 'She acted like my best friend and at school she wouldn't be seen dead with me.'

'Really? I don't get you girls, sometimes. I could have sworn when she first came over that you really liked each other.'

'Hmm, sometimes you have to fake it for an easy life,' I say, and I feel a stab of guilt at the knowledge that I'm faking it with him too. But I'm not being two-faced like Lisa. I *do* like Max, I'm just waiting for the chemistry to happen. And it will. Soon. I'm sure.

We have a wonderful day. Max and I stuff ourselves with free drink and food and ice cream, and he even buys me some freshly spun candy floss from a stall. I've tried on vintage clothes and jewellery, watched acrobats and dancers, and bounced up and down on a giant trampoline. The sun is beating down and the air is thick with the smell of sun cream and delicious food. I can't remember ever having this much fun. It feels like going to the best shopping centre, visiting the circus and going to a theme park all at the same time. Some of the other bands are really good, even the ones I've never heard of, and in between I'm loving hanging around the VIP area, waiting to see who walks in. If I had anyone to play the Celebometer with, my points would be going off the scale today. I've seen TV presenters and actors and models, as well as rock stars, and I know some of them have been looking at me and wondering who I am too. I've been playing it really cool, of course, trying not to react or appear starstruck. I just smile at them, enigmatically, as if I know them from somewhere, but can't quite place them.

It's getting dark now and it will soon be time for Fieldstar to start their set. We're lying in the grass, at right angles to each other, my head on Max's chest. He's stroking my hair with one hand, and my arm with the other. It feels comfortable, not exciting or thrilling, but lovely, as if I'm safe and cared for. I feel like I want to give him a great big bear hug.

'I wish this wasn't just a one-day thing,' says Max. 'It would be fun to camp out with you.'

'Yeah,' I say. 'But Mum and Dad would never let me. Not unless I shared with Isabella and you shared with Rufus, and there was a padlock on the tent.'

'Hmm,' he says. 'Although Rufus would get his own

hotel room. The bands don't have to camp. Which is a good thing, as I could never share a tent with him. God, no.'

'Why not?'

He pauses for a second. 'Rufus has a terrible sleepwalking problem,' he says, quietly. 'Don't tell anyone, but when we were younger he used to get into all kinds of fixes. Once, we found him wandering naked in the garden. Another time, he tried to climb out of his window. He doesn't remember anything about it the next day and he's really embarrassed about it; it's like our big family secret. I don't think he's so bad any more, but if you check out his bedroom window you'll see it's fixed so it doesn't open much, just in case.'

'Wow,' I say. 'Course I won't tell anyone. Poor Rufus.'

'Yeah. I think the drumming helps. That's kind of why he started doing it. He was hyperactive as a kid and my parents thought that if he used up some of his energy he might stop sleepwalking.'

'Wow, so Fieldstar wouldn't exist if Rufus didn't sleepwalk?'

'No, probably not. You won't say anything, will you?' he says. 'He'd hate it if it got out.'

'Course not. Who am I going to tell?'

Max strokes my cheek and props himself up on his elbow. 'Come on, then,' he says. 'Let's go and find our places for Fieldstar. Isabella promised she'd reserve a good spot for us.'

Fieldstar play the best gig they've ever played. To be fair, it's only the second time I've seen them live, so I can't be certain, but they do keep saying it and telling us – the crowd – that we're the best audience they've ever seen or heard, and that we're all beautiful, so it must be true. They play a storming hour-long set, with all their big anthems, plus a few tracks from the new album, the one Dad is designing the cover for. At first, I feel self-conscious singing along because I'm not just a fan any more, I'm a friend. And I'm standing right next to Mick Jagger, who doesn't seem to be enjoying it all that much. But it's dark and there are thousands of people singing and waving their arms, and soon I don't care; I just let the music and the atmosphere carry me away. I feel so relaxed and happy that when Max grabs me and plants a smacker of a kiss on my lips, I almost *want* to kiss him back.

Chapter 17

He Loves Me . . .
Oh God!

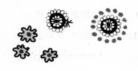

till half-asleep, I'm just logging on to my email, when an instant message pops up from Sky.

Sky: *Rosie, thank God you're there!*

Me: *Hey, Sky, it's so good to hear from you. So you found an internet café then? How's it going?*

Sky: *Honestly? I'm going crazy. This place is filled with wall to wall flakes. My mum is loving it!*

Me: *Oh you poor thing.*

Sky: *Yeah, the only good thing is I'm getting an awesome tan. How's things with you?*

Me: *Good . . . ish. Went to the G Festival yesterday with Max. I was on the guest list!*

Sky: *I am so jealous! Who did you see?*

Me: *Loads of people. Don't even know all their names. Everyone you've ever heard of was there.*

Sky: *Everyone? Was Adam Grigson there?*

Me: *No, apart from him. Shame. Maybe he's gone back home now. I've been looking out for him in coffee shops but I haven't seen him again, worse luck. I tell you who was there, though — not a celebrity — Lisa, this really bitchy girl from school. She was waiting outside the VIP area and she tried to make out she was my best mate, just so I'd get her in too. Can you believe it?*

Sky: *You crack me up! Rosie, you do realise that if you didn't know Max that would have been you, don't you? You'd have been hanging around outside the VIP area, desperate to see someone you knew so you could get in too!*

Me: *God, I guess you're right. How embarrassing. I never looked at it like that. Am I that pathetic?*

Sky: *Don't worry, I'd have been right there with you. So what's the goss?*

Me: *Nothing really. Been seeing a lot of Max. Still not 100% about him. Sorry, I know that's boring. Oh, and I've made up with Vix, although it's a bit weird still. Um, other than that, nothing really.*

Sky: *Go on, you must have something interesting to tell me. Please! I am sooooo bored here. I need something to keep me going.*

I ponder her request. I could fill her in about Rufus, but I promised Max I wouldn't tell anyone. Then again, I tell Sky everything. And she's thousands of miles away at a meditation retreat. Who is she going to tell? The yogi?

Me: *Welllll I did find something out about Rufus, something nobody else knows . . .*

Sky: *Yeah? Go on . . .*

Me: *OK, this is a secret, yeah? Rufus sleepwalks. He's got a real problem. He climbs out of windows and goes wandering around the garden stark naked.*

Sky: *Seriously?*

Me: *Yeah, Max says he started doing it when they were kids.*

From downstairs I can hear the buzz of the doorbell. I'm still in my nightie and I'm not expecting anyone. I really don't want to have to break off my conversation and go downstairs to open the door. What if it's Rufus? Not that he's ever popped round unexpectedly before. He's probably still at the after-show party, the one I had to leave before it had barely begun just so Mum and Dad could see I was home safely. I glance in the mirror on my dressing table. I look a mess, with last night's mascara smeared down my cheeks. Someone else can get the door.

Sky: *Have you seen him do it – wandering around the garden naked?*

There's that annoying buzz again, more persistent this

time. I check my watch: it's eleven-thirty. Mum will be at work and, now that I think about it, Dad said he was taking Charlie to some summer holiday sports activity day. He won't be back for at least half an hour. I'm the only one in.

Me: *Hang on, Sky, I just need to get the door.*

I stuff my feet into my slippers and rush downstairs, two steps at a time. Through the frosted glass I can make out the shape of a large man, wearing what looks like a motorbike helmet. He's carrying something big, in both arms. I put the door on the chain, like Mum told me to do, and peer around it. 'Hello?'

'Delivery for Rosie Buttery. Needs to be signed for.'

For me? I can't remember the last time I had a delivery. I don't remember ordering anything online, and it isn't my birthday for months. 'Hold on . . .' I'm excited now: what can it be? I grab Dad's overcoat from the coat rack and put it on over my nightie. Then I take the door off the chain and cautiously open it a little wider.

'Miss Buttery?' The courier is about twenty and very cute. And here I am in my nightie. I haven't even cleaned my teeth. How embarrassing.

'That's me. Although I don't normally look like this. Had a late night, you see.'

'Right. Er, would you like to sign here, please?'

'Sure!' I have a great signature. I've practised it endlessly, ready for the day when I'm famous and known as Rosie B and have to sign autographs. I present him with my best squiggle – with a smiley face inside the 'o' – and, nodding, he hands over the giant box. 'Ooh, do you know what it is?' I ask.

'No idea,' he says. 'All I know is it was a bugger to carry on my bike. The van is out of action today. Enjoy.'

'Oh, sorry. And thanks.'

He nods and disappears up the garden path, while I shut the front door and wrestle with the giant cardboard box in the hallway. It says, *Fragile, Keep Upright* on it, but it doesn't weigh much. I can't find any scissors, so I rip it open with the heel of one of Mum's shoes, so excited that I almost forget to breathe. Inside is an enormous bouquet of slightly crushed red and pink flowers, a box of chocolates (the praline sort, that I don't really like) and a small, soft, yellow teddy bear, with a tiny envelope attached to it. I pull out the card.

To Rosie,
Thanks for making yesterday so special.
I've been to hundreds of Fieldstar gigs, but this was the first
one I've really enjoyed.
Can't wait to see you again,
Love, Max xxxx

Oh wow! This is the most romantic thing anyone has ever done for me. Nobody – certainly no boy – has ever sent me flowers, or chocolates or a teddy bear. And even though it's clichéd and a little bit naff, and the teddy bear is cross-eyed, and I'll be giving Mum the chocolates, and I will probably kill the flowers before they're even in the vase, I feel an overwhelming sense of happiness. I feel special. I don't think I've ever felt special before.

I rush upstairs, leaving the gifts and the torn box on the floor in the hall, and, as fast as I can type, send Max a text: *Thk u so mch 4 pressies. Ur so swt. xxxxx*

It's only at this point that I remember I was in the middle of a conversation with Sky. The message box is still up, but under Sky's name it reads, *User not online*. What a shame. I'd love to tell her about Max's gifts and see what she thinks, but now I've no way of contacting her. And I have no idea when she'll next be online. It could be days.

I read back over our conversation and realise I didn't tell her, on pain of death, not to tell anyone about Rufus. I said it was a big secret, but perhaps I should have spelled it out. Still, she'll get it, won't she? And, as I said, she's in Goa, she can't tell anyone. I'm sure there's no harm done.

I hear the rattle of a key in the front door. Dad must be home. 'Rosie?' he calls up the stairs. 'You up?'

'Yes, Dad, just,' I say, walking out of my bedroom, so he can see me at the top of the stairs. 'Just coming.'

'What's all this in the hall?'

'Hang on . . .' I walk back downstairs. 'They're presents. For me! I was about to come down and sort them out. Sorry about the mess.'

'Hmm, you'd better do, before your mum gets home. Presents? From whom?'

'From Max,' I say, and as I say it, I can't help thinking I wish the gifts were from someone else.

'Oh, darling! How wonderful.'

'I know! Sweet, isn't it? He's so generous and thoughtful.'

'Looks like more than that to me,' says Dad. He looks at me weirdly, almost as if he's seeing me for the first time.

'What do you mean?'

'I would have thought it was obvious,' says Dad. 'He's falling in love with you. A boy wouldn't make a grand gesture like that unless he was.'

Oh God! Oh God! Oh God!

'Really? Are you sure?'

I must visibly crumple up because Dad looks concerned. 'What's wrong love?'

'But I'm not in love with *him*, Dad. I don't think I ever will be. I've been trying, for ages now, to make myself do something more than *like* Max, to want to be more than his best friend, and it's just not happening.' I feel I should explain about the kissing, to make it clearer, but that's really not something I can talk to my dad about.

'Sometimes it takes time,' he says.

'How much time? I don't have time. Not if you're right and he's fallen in love with me already.'

'Well, if you're really sure that you don't want to be more than friends, there's only one thing you can do. The kind thing. You need to end it now, before it gets out of hand.'

'But he'll be gutted! I don't want to hurt him. Maybe

he won't even want to be my friend any more.'

'You'll hurt him more the longer you leave it. Yes, he'll be upset, but if he's as nice a guy as he seems, he'll be a gentleman about it, I'm sure.'

'And I'm his "plus one" at Fieldstar gigs. I won't be able to go if I dump him. Rufus might hate me too. And what about the big album launch gig at KOKO? I've been looking forward to that more than anything.'

'You can't have it both ways, love,' says Dad. 'You can't just go out with Max because he's Rufus's brother.'

'I know that.' I do know that. I also know what I have to do. So why does something so clear and simple feel so complicated and difficult? Maybe, if I think really hard, I can come up with a plan B.

Chapter 18

A Foolproof Plan

My plan B is simple and it's genius: rather than dumping Max and breaking his heart, which will probably mean he doesn't want to see me or speak to me ever again, I'm going to go all out to make him go off me. Then, he'll dump me instead. And, being such a gentleman, I'm fairly sure that he won't be spiteful enough to take away my guest list ticket for the gig at KOKO. He'll see it as my consolation prize.

The idea came to me last night in bed, while I was lying awake wracking my brains for a solution – just like I've been doing every night for the past week. It's a perfect plan: nobody gets hurt. I really can't fault it. I'm telling Vix all about it now. It feels so good to be (nearly) straight with her at last and to get everything off my chest, to talk to her in a way I haven't been able to since the whole Max business began. I can almost see the Max-shaped block between us disintegrating before my eyes, chunk by chunk, like *Tetris* in reverse.

'I've missed you so much, Vix,' I tell her, hugging her for about the hundredth time. We're sitting in her bedroom, drinking hot chocolate and eating home-made brownies. 'Although I really do hate the fact that you're always right!'

'I've missed you too, Rosie,' she says, hugging me back. 'And I'm so pleased you're finally being honest with me – and yourself – but . . .'

There's always a 'but' with Vix.

'. . . but I'm not sure you're going about it the right way. It's kind of a bit . . . manipulative, isn't it? I mean, if you've decided you definitely don't want to be with him, then shouldn't you just be honest with him and call it quits, instead of playing games?'

'Yeah, but, it's much less painful this way.' I don't mention the wanting to stay on the KOKO guest list bit; she wouldn't approve. I need her to think I'm being totally unselfish, or she might stop talking to me again. 'It's kinder.'

'Maybe. So what are you going to do to put him off you? Stop shaving your legs? Forget to clean your teeth?'

'Yeah, they're two of the options. I've started making a list.'

'Rosie! I was kidding.'

'Oh, right.'

She laughs. 'So what else is on this list, then?'

I tell her. My list, entitled *Ways To Make Max Go Off Me,* contains the following:

1) Stop shaving my legs.

2) Stop wearing make-up.

3) Only clean my teeth at night, and never before I see Max.

4) Chew gum. With my mouth open. All the time. (The fruit-flavoured sort, so it doesn't cancel out the non teeth-brushing.)

5) Wear baggy clothes.

6) Develop some sort of nervous tic. A twitch, maybe? Or something really annoying, like constantly clicking my fingers or going cross-eyed.

7) Develop an interest in something incredibly boring, like bird-watching, and talk about it non-stop.

8) Yawn whenever Max starts talking about graphic novels, or manga, etc.

9) Check out other guys in front of him. (I might not go through with this one, because it's too cruel. I don't need Vix to point that out for me.)

10) Start being a little bit unreliable: turning up late, not ringing back or texting back straightaway, etc.

There's also a number eleven, and it's one I don't tell Vix about:

11) Talk about how great Vix is all the time, involve her in as many of our plans as possible, and try to make him start fancying her instead. Result: a happy ending for everyone.

'So,' says Vix, 'you're going to give up on personal hygiene, turn into the wild woman of Camden Town and entirely change your personality. Hmm, have you thought what might happen if it doesn't work, and he still likes you?'

No, I haven't thought about that. My plan is foolproof. Isn't it?

I guess I'll find out soon enough, because we're meeting Max in a few minutes. We're jumping on the tube and going into London to see some of the sights. It only takes about fifteen minutes to get to Leicester Square station from Camden Town and the plan is to do Covent Garden, Trafalgar Square, Piccadilly Circus and The Mall, which runs up to Buckingham Palace, like the Queen's personal, very grand driveway. Max hasn't been to London properly since he was a kid, so he wants to do the whole tourist bit. He doesn't seem to mind that I've invited Vix too, although he did say he'd like to spend some 'alone' time with me later.

I open the front door to him, dressed in old jeans that don't really fit and a shapeless sweatshirt. I haven't done anything with my hair and I'm not wearing a scrap of make-up.

'You look different,' he says. 'I can't work it out.' He studies my face. 'I know what it is – you're not wearing that black eyeliner you usually wear. You look fresh – natural. I like it.'

Vix catches my eye. Her expression reads: Well, that's backfired on you, hasn't it?

This isn't going to be as easy as I hoped. Next time I see Max, I shall have to dress as a full-blown Emo.

We take the tube to Leicester Square and walk down Charing Cross Road to Trafalgar Square, where we perch on the side of one of the fountains. It's a glorious day and it's packed with backpacking tourists admiring the scenery. I act disinterested, like I've seen it all before (which I have), check my phone constantly and try not to engage in conversation with Max. He doesn't look irritated; he looks concerned.

'You OK?' he whispers. He's already asked twice.

'Course I am. I'm just tired.'

'You sure?'

'Yes,' I snap. I'm not annoyed with him; I'm annoyed with myself for being mean. 'Look at all those tourists. Vix has travelled loads, haven't you Vix?' I say, changing the subject and my tack. 'Tell him about when you went to the States. Max has been to America too, haven't you, Max?'

Max nods and smiles. 'Which bits have you visited, Vix?' he says.

'I've got family in New York and I've been to LA, San Francisco, Washington, all over really.'

'Yeah, me too. I went to a ranch in Texas last summer – I got to do real Wild West horse riding. No saddles.'

'Really?' says Vix, who used to be pony mad when we were kids. 'Cool. I used to ride a lot when I was younger . . .'

Anyone can see that Vix has got so much more in common with Max than I have. Maybe he'll start to realise that soon, and then . . . Right, now they're talking, it's time to leave them to it for a while. 'Sorry to interrupt, but I just need to pop to the loo,' I say. 'Won't be five minutes.' I start walking away.

'You sure you don't want me to come too?' says Vix.

'Nah, I'll be fine, there's one right over there.' I point to the café building. 'See you in a tick.'

I take far longer than five minutes. After I've been to the loo, and despaired at my make-up-free reflection in the mirror, I go into the café and queue up to buy a bottle of water. On the way out, I notice a small group of protestors, standing around faded pictures of Chinese people and passing around a petition. It's something to do with fighting human rights abuses in China. I sign my best squiggle and pause to read about the people who've been arrested and tortured or killed. It makes me think how lucky I am to have been born in London. The biggest problem in my life is how to get rid of a lovely guy who really cares about me. How unfair is that?

Max and Vix are still immersed in their conversation when I arrive back. They're laughing so much that it takes them a minute to realise that I'm standing there. I don't feel the slightest bit jealous, I feel pleased, and it makes me certain I'm doing the right thing.

'Hey,' says Max, reaching for my hand. 'You OK?'

'Sure,' I say, reluctantly allowing him to take it and trying to avoid Vix's eye. 'I'm good. Where shall we go next?'

'Let's go to see the Queen,' he says. 'If she's in.'

'Course she is. I told her we were coming.'

We have fun the rest of the afternoon, seeing the sites and eating ice cream in Leicester Square. Keeping the plan going is exhausting and I keep lapsing into being myself and enjoying Max's company. But then Vix says she needs to head back and Max says he wants to buy me dinner. Before I know it, I'm left alone with him again in a boyfriend-girlfriend situation, and I can't pretend that he's just a mate and that everything is normal.

We go to a cheap Italian chain restaurant. I order garlic bread and a pizza, with extra onions. If Max minds, he certainly doesn't show it. He polishes off his own meal and half of mine, making his breath equally stinky. He even says something about how great it is that I have a healthy appetite and I'm not one of those girls who's constantly on a diet and only eats salad. Arghh!

Afterwards, we wander into Piccadilly Circus and look for somewhere to sit down. We've just found a spot when I look up and realise we're sitting right by the famous statue of Eros. Eros is only the Greek god of *love*. Max is bound to know that. We have got to get out of here before he spots it and goes all romantic on me!

'Let's go to the Trocadero,' I suggest. 'I've suddenly got loads of energy again. It's fun. You'll love it.'

I'm lying. The Trocadero is not that much fun. It's, frankly, a bit rubbish. It's a grand building that Mum told me used to be a restaurant, but now it's run-down and full of touristy-shops, selling models of London buses, posters and pick and mixes. There's also an entertainment centre, where you can play video games, go bowling or ride on the dodgems. After my stodgy meal, I'm too stuffed for pick and mix or bumper cars, so we play a couple of arcade games and then browse in the shops. One of them has a whole section devoted to Adam Grigson, with out-of-date calendars (it's August), souvenir books and postcards.

'Oh wow, I love Adam Grigson. He is *so* my type,' I say, dropping Max's hand and picking up a postcard showing Adam Grigson without his shirt. The words have just popped out of my mouth. It's not as cruel as checking out a real, flesh-and-blood guy in front of him, but I know it's still a mean thing to do. It must be obvious to Max that Adam Grigson is physically his polar opposite. I know I wouldn't like it if I was out on a date and the boy said, 'Oh, I love tall, skinny blondes with big boobs.'

Max looks confused, then slightly wounded. 'Let me buy it for you,' he says.

Why does he always have to be so *nice*? 'No, you really shouldn't. I can get it myself. And I don't really need it.'

'I want to. I insist. I like buying you presents.' Before I can argue again, he heads off to the till, the photo in his hand. It's as if he's paying for me to slap him in the face. I feel like the biggest bitch in the world.

He comes back, not only with the picture, but with a stupid keyring with a photo of Adam Grigson in full vampire get-up on it. 'Thought you'd like this too,' he says. 'To add to your collection.'

'Thanks,' I say, and I know I don't sound very grateful.

'Don't you mean *fangs*?'

I smile, in spite of myself. 'Very funny. But you really shouldn't have bought that for me. Why do you always have to be so generous? It's too much.' I know I sound cold and he looks hurt again.

'What's with you today? You've been really weird with me, blowing hot and cold. Have I done something?'

'No,' I say. And then I deliver the most pathetic, clichéd line in the book. 'It's not you, OK? It's me.'

'OK,' he says, softly. 'Why don't we go home? I'm sure you'll feel better tomorrow.'

'I don't think so,' I mutter, under my breath.

'I just want to get a drink for the journey,' he says, trying to sound bright. 'Want one? Let's go and find a shop that's still open.'

We walk back through Trafalgar Square and up Charing Cross Road in silence. Just before the tube station, we find one of those newsagent/grocery stores that sells everything at inflated prices. I follow Max inside and loiter by the checkout, while he goes to find some cans of Coke in the fridge.

He's on his way towards me with the drinks when I spot something that makes my stomach helter-skelter into my feet. There on the counter, where it can't be missed, is a pile of copies of *Sizzling*, the biggest-selling gossip magazine in the country. And, unmistakably, taking up almost the whole of the front cover, is a huge and rather unflattering picture of Rufus Justice. The headline reads: *Fieldstar Drummer in Nude Garden Shocker!*

Chapter 19

What Have I Done?

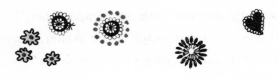

There's a whooshing sound in my ears and all at once it feels like everything is happening in slow motion. Max is coming towards me, smiling, with two cans of Coke in his hands, and I know that when he reaches me – in four seconds, three seconds, two seconds . . . my life will be over. He hasn't seen the magazine yet but he's going to. It's a one hundred per cent certainty. Even if I had the time, I couldn't possibly buy every copy in the shop. And there will be more copies in other shops – copies in every newsagent in London and in every newsagent in the country. *Sizzling* sells millions. Worse, it won't be long before other magazines and newspapers start picking up the story and spinning it into whatever they want. I know how this works: I've seen it happen a thousand times.

'Max . . .' I say, desperately. 'There's something you should know . . .'

But it's too late. He's reached the counter and spotted the magazine. His face is white with shock and he looks shaky and breathless. Slamming down the drinks, he picks up the magazine for a closer look. Then, in an expressionless voice, he says, 'And the magazine, please,' to the shopkeeper. He hands over a ten pound note and, without waiting for his change, rushes towards me, grabbing my arm and almost marches me to the door.

'Oh my God,' he says. 'This is really bad. Really bad. Got to get home.' He practically runs to the tube station, forcing me to jog to keep up with him, and then he's through the barrier and speeding down the escalator, two steps at a time. We reach the platform and jump on to a northbound tube just before the doors close. Once we're sitting down, and the tube has moved off, he catches his breath. Then he thumbs through the magazine, clumsily, until he finds the page where the story is printed in full. Holding my breath, I peer over his shoulder to read it too.

Fieldstar Full Frontal Garden Scandal!

Rufus Justice has shocked his neighbours in trendy Camden Town by stripping off and wandering around his garden starkers in the middle of the night. The exuberant Fieldstar

*drummer was seen naked in his garden at 3 a.m. last week,
according to a source, thought to be a friend. 'He's been sleepwalking since he was a kid, it's a real problem,' the source told
us. 'There are several young families on the street and the
neighbours aren't happy.'*

*We thought that Justice, who used to be known for his
wild ways, had calmed down since meeting stunning Russian
model Isabella Primanova two years ago. Sounds to us like
he's back to his old tricks . . .*

With every word I read, my heart rate speeds up by
another five beats, until I start to feel sick and breathless.
It's bad enough that Rufus's embarrassing problem is out
in public; worse, the article makes him sound like some
sort of pervert who enjoys stripping off in his garden in
the middle of the night. The sleepwalking part is hidden in
the middle – you'd barely notice it if you weren't reading
closely. And they've got all the facts wrong! Isabella isn't
Russian – she's Czech. And she's not a model. And who is
the source it mentions? I know it's not me. It can't be Max,
or Isabella, or the guys in Fieldstar. The timing is too much
of a coincidence for there to be any other possible
explanation: Sky must have told someone what I told her;
who, I can't imagine. And then that someone must have
told someone else, who told the magazine. And probably
got paid loads for the story too! But whichever way I look
at it, it's still my fault. *What have I done?*

Max stares at me, steely-eyed. I know he's asking himself exactly the same questions as me, coming to the same conclusions at exactly the same time. He sighs and takes my hand. 'Rosie, I don't want to have to ask you this, but I have to know. Was it you? Did you tell someone? Because you're the only person I've ever told. I can't figure out how else it's got out. It's been a secret for years.' He pauses. 'I really hope it wasn't you.'

I can't look at him. I want the tube to stop in a tunnel and leave me there, in the dark, on my own, for ever. 'I'm so, so sorry,' I mutter. 'I didn't mean to.'

He drops my hand. 'I know you wouldn't sell the story. Would you? So who did you tell?'

'Only Sky. We tell each other everything. I know that's no excuse. But she's in Goa. And I can usually trust her. Please don't blame her, because it's my fault. I shouldn't have said anything. I'm so, so sorry.'

I want him to be angry with me, but he isn't. He doesn't shout or walk away; he just looks at me with sad, watery eyes, as though he's disappointed and I'm not the person he thought I was. 'It's not your fault,' he says, softly. 'It's totally my fault. Rufus always said I shouldn't trust anyone. The rules are different when you're a celebrity. I shouldn't have told you.' He turns away from me and stares blankly out the tube window, as the tunnel walls rush past.

I've been trying all day to make him go off me. And now he has. So why don't I feel good about it?

Chapter 20

Paparazzi on Paradise Avenue

Rufus Justice is depressed. He hasn't come out of his house for six days, not once, since the story about his sleepwalking broke. He can't even go in his own back garden because most of the paparazzi lenses are trained on it, hoping to catch him in the buff. Max says he just sits in the living room with the curtains shut, wearing his dressing gown and playing on his Wii. He hasn't even touched his drums or picked up a pen to scribble down a song idea. Isabella is going spare and the other Fieldstar members are worried sick that Rufus won't be able to play the gig at KOKO, which is only days away now.

I feel so bad that I've offered to go round to explain

what happened and to say sorry to Rufus, but Max said not to. He's such a gentleman that he hasn't told his brother I'm to blame. Rufus has no clue how the story got out, and now he probably never will. It will just remain a 'mystery'. Max says it's better that way.

'Rufus doesn't really trust anyone anyway,' Max explained. 'Where the story came from isn't important now. The fact is it's out and it can't ever go back in.'

The day after *Sizzling* hit the shops, two of the tabloid newspapers picked up on it and it spread all over the internet too. People have been posting really mean pictures showing a naked, fat guy with Rufus's head pasted over the top, and telling incredibly mean jokes, like saying *they* have no trouble sleeping properly when they listen to Fieldstar's albums. Fieldstar had a meeting with their management team and it was decided that they'd do something called 'fire fighting'. Now they're trying to turn the negative story into a positive one. So, reluctantly, Rufus has done interviews with newspaper health sections and on the radio about his sleepwalking problem, and how it isn't funny at all. It's actually a serious medical condition that can be really dangerous. One paper said some people have hurt themselves or their partners while they were asleep. Not that Rufus has ever done this. The line is he wants to help other people with the same problem.

I used to think celebrity gossip was exciting. But all the fuss has made me realise that being famous can be rubbish sometimes. I'd hate to be Rufus now, stuck in my house, with photographers and journalists ready to pounce at any opportunity. No one cares that he's a real person, with real feelings.

I've been trying to do some fire fighting of my own. I've put my Max plan on hold, for starters. It feels mean and petty now. And the truth is, I think he's gone off me a little bit anyway – it's obvious, however sweet he's being. It feels like he doesn't really trust me any more. He hasn't said anything, but he's stopped being so open with me and so affectionate and, because he's worried about Rufus, he's been spending a lot of time at home and not coming out very much. The few times he's kissed me, I've just closed my eyes and thought about Adam Grigson. Until all the fuss has died down, I don't see how I can do anything else. I'm stuck with him as my boyfriend.

The night I saw the magazine, I rushed off an email to Sky the minute I got home. I was hoping she'd see it quickly and fill me in on what happened. A tiny part of me was praying that maybe, just maybe, she'd swear she hadn't told a soul and the whole thing really was a massive coincidence, so I could stop blaming myself. Either way, just sending it made me feel better.

Dear Sky,

Oh God! What a mess!

Rufus is all over the news in England. Have you heard?

God, not sure how to say this but was it you? Did you

mention it to somebody? There's this 'source' and no one knows who they are. I know I should have made it crystal clear that you weren't supposed to tell anyone about the sleepwalking, but I thought you'd realise that without me saying. I'm not blaming you, but it's really dropped me in it. Who did you tell? How did it end up in a magazine? I want to die! PLEASE email me or call me as soon as you can.

Love, Rosie x

I haven't heard from her. Maybe she hasn't been able to go online, or maybe she's too shamefaced to answer me. She's coming back from Goa in a few days, so I'll be able to ask her what happened, face to face.

I'm with Vix right now in a café on Camden High Street, eating strawberry and white chocolate muffins and drinking iced chocolate frappés. Her treat. We're sitting in our favourite spot, right by the window, watching people go by. People, not celebrities. I've packed the Celebometer away for now, maybe for keeps. It doesn't feel fun any more. It's how I got myself into this mess in the first place!

This time I've been totally straight with Vix. I confessed what I'd done and she has been surprisingly sweet about everything. She says she'd have done exactly the same thing – told me or Sky – about Rufus's sleepwalking, if she'd been Max's girlfriend.

'It's not really breaking a promise to tell your best

friend something because there's an unwritten code, isn't there?' she says. 'Everyone knows it. Talking to your best friend is a bit like thinking aloud.'

'Except Sky told someone else.'

'Yeah, but like you said, you didn't tell her how important it was not to, and she was probably going crazy out there with no news and no gossip. She's going to feel terrible when she finds out what trouble she's caused.'

'Yeah,' I say, although I think that, secretly, Sky will also feel quite proud to have started such a fuss. She doesn't know Rufus like I do.

'Everyone will forget about it soon, though. There'll be some other celebrity scandal to talk about.'

'Yeah,' I say. 'I know. But the stuff about Rufus will always be on the web now. And he wanted to keep it private. Anyway, want another drink?'

'What do you think? Course I do.'

'I'll get them this time.'

There's a long queue, mainly because the guy serving – I think they call them baristas – is a bit hopeless and keeps getting the orders wrong or giving people the wrong change. I lean against the counter, impatiently, thinking, 'Hurry up, already.'

'God,' says a voice from behind me. 'We'll still be here for breakfast at this rate.'

I turn around. It's a guy, a year or two older than me, perhaps, and he's absolutely gorgeous, with dark hair flopping over one eye and a slim, muscular body. He looks like he should be in a band. But probably isn't.

'Yeah, tell me about it,' I say, trying not to blush. I suddenly feel self-conscious. I check out my reflection in the cake counter. I think I look OK. Thank goodness I put the plan on hold and started wearing make-up and dressing like me again.

'It's always the same here,' he says. 'Always too packed. So are you a tourist visiting the market?'

'As if! No, I've lived in Camden all my life. I'm a local. You?'

'Yeah, I live here too. Well, Chalk Farm, officially. Just the other end of the high street.'

'Oh right, I'm up by the Camden Road end.'

He smiles and holds out his hand. He is soooo my type. 'I'm Laurie, by the way.'

'Rosie,' I say, shaking it. I hope my palms aren't too sweaty.

The queue still isn't moving much. I try to catch Vix's eye, but she's sitting with her back towards me.

'You here with a friend?'

'Yeah, my best friend, Vix. She's just over there.' I point to the back of Vix's head. 'We always sit in the window seats. Best place for people-watching. You?'

'Just getting a takeaway. I'm doing a summer job at the sports shop on the high street. I'm on my break.' He checks his watch. 'At least I was.'

'You can go in front of me, if you like.'

'Ah, you're very sweet, but don't worry. If I'm late, I'm late.'

By the time I've picked up my drinks, I've found out quite a lot about Laurie. It turns out he's just about to start sixth form. He has a sister in my year at school and he's been to some of the same gigs as me. He's so easy to talk to, and so cute, I almost forget I'm standing in a public queue with a stranger. And I almost forget I have a boyfriend.

'So,' says Laurie, as he collects his own drink. 'I have to get back to work now.' He pauses. 'I'm, er, not normally this forward but, er, do you fancy meeting up some time? Could I take your number? I would ask you out for a coffee, but as we're already in a café that sounds a bit stupid.'

'Oh . . .' I can feel my face fall.

'Sorry,' he says, with a forced smile. 'You don't have to give it to me. I shouldn't have asked.'

'No, it's not that. I'd love to give you my number. But I really can't. I have a, er, boyfriend.' I want to add, 'I'm working on it,' but that would make me sound really mean.

'Shame,' he says. 'Maybe some other time.'

'Maybe,' I say.

'See you around, then.' He smiles and turns and I watch him walk out of the cafe.

I feel gutted. And, once again, I've got no one to blame but myself.

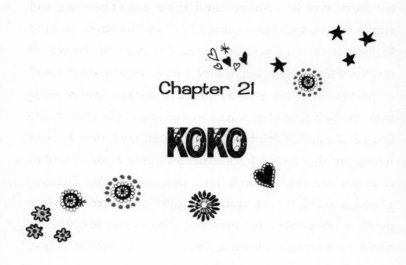

Chapter 21

KOKO

Last night, Fieldstar launched their brand new album at KOKO with a one-off gig. People queued around the block from five in the morning, camping out, hoping that they would be lucky enough to buy one of the small number of public tickets available. Everybody else was on the guest list: friends and family, rock stars, TV presenters and footballers, as well as journalists and people from Fieldstar's record company. It was a real dress-up occasion, like a film première, and Isabella looked incredible, in a beautiful sea-green silk dress. Guests drank free champagne and cocktails and ate mini burgers in toy-sized buns, or tiny portions of fish and chips from cardboard cones. Afterwards, there was a big party, which went on until three a.m. There are still empty bottles and bits of tinsel littering the streets around KOKO. Everybody is saying it was the event of the year, if not the decade. Then again, they always say that, don't they?

Maybe he's just a really good actor, but you'd never have guessed that Rufus had any troubles. He even made a joke about his 'problem' and announced that he was setting up the 'Rufus Justice Sleepwalking Foundation' to raise money for research into sleep disorders. Fieldstar played a stonking set and their new album tracks went down a treat with the audience. The critics loved them too. One journalist blogged, *Tonight saw the birth of a classic album from Britain's best-loved band.*

But the best moment of all was when Rufus unveiled the new album, on stage, and said it was called *The Tarantula*. Guess what: the sleeve features Dad's painting, *The Quiet Death of the Tarantula*. Dad is so proud. And I'm so proud of him. His little squiggle of a signature is there, in the corner, on every copy. Fieldstar have put the album out on vinyl, as well as on CD and download, so true fans will be able to see Dad's work on a proper scale. Dad says that Rufus liked his original ideas for the album cover but kept coming back to the *Tarantula* painting, which Dad brought round to show him after Rufus had admired a photo of it on his phone. 'It has such power, such tranquility,' he told Dad. 'I think we all feel like that tarantula, dying quietly on the beach, don't we?'

I have absolutely no idea what he was talking about. Still,

who cares? Dad is so happy he looks like he's going to burst. This may only be the second painting he's ever sold, and Mum says he shouldn't have done another 'mates rates' deal with Rufus, but it's going to be seen by millions of people, all over the world. My dad is going to be famous. Kind of.

I can't tell you how much I wish I could have been there last night to see it all, to be part of it. But I didn't go to KOKO. I only know what happened because I've read some of it on the internet and Vix has filled me in on the rest. I didn't go because yesterday morning, I woke up and, for the first time in my life, I was one hundred per cent certain of what I had to do. I had my plan C.

'Muuuuuum,' I called out, in a cracking voice. 'I don't feel well. Please come.' I wrapped myself up tight in my duvet and tried to look sweaty and pale.

Mum came in, looking concerned, in her officious doctor's way. 'What's wrong, Rosie?'

'I feel awful,' I said. 'I've got a terrible fever and my muscles hurt, and I've got a headache and a cough, and the runs, and I'm all sweaty too. And then I go all cold.' Those are the symptoms of a disease that Katy Kay, from my favourite girl band, Proud Girls, had when she came back from Africa. I remember reading about them.

'Sounds like you're a bit flu-y,' Mum said, suspiciously. 'Unusual in August. But possible. You're probably just coming down with a cold.'

'Oh no, it's not a cold. It's much worse than that,' I

whined. I remembered some of the other symptoms. 'My eyes hurt and I've got a bit of a rash too.'

'Let me look.' She opened the duvet and I did my best impression of a shiver. 'I can't see anything.'

'My joints hurt too.'

'Rosie, I'm sure you don't feel well, but I think you've been reading my medical encyclopaedia again. You've just listed all the symptoms of dengue fever.'

'Yes, that's it. That's what I've got.' That's exactly what Katy Kay had! I remembered. She was bitten by a mosquito on holiday, and that's what caused it.

'I've been bitten by a mosquito,' I said. 'Look.' I showed Mum a little midge bite on my leg. 'This must be it. I got bitten on Primrose Hill the other day.'

She sighed. 'Rosie, you can't get dengue fever in England, and certainly not on Primrose Hill. It's a tropical disease. The mosquitoes here don't carry it.'

'What about climate change?' I asked. 'It's been a very hot summer.'

'It's not dengue fever,' said Mum. 'Believe me. But I'll take your temperature anyway, just to be sure you are OK.'

She went out of the room and came back in with the thermometer. Fortunately it was the one that you stick under your tongue, not the one you put in your bottom. She's given me that one before, when she suspected me of faking illness to avoid school. 'Now open your mouth and say ahhh.'

'Ahhhh.'

'Right, I'll be back in a minute. And no putting it on the radiator or in a cup of tea while I'm out the room.' Damn my mother, I thought, she knows all the tricks.

I lay in bed, patiently, with the thermometer balanced under my tongue, waiting for Mum to return. She came back in with a glass of water and slid the thermometer out of my mouth. 'Your temperature is actually up slightly,' she said, with a hint of surprise. 'Maybe you really are ill.'

Really? Result, I thought. It must be the anxiety. I've worried myself sick, literally.

'Best thing to do is stay in bed today and rest. Lots of fluids. Then we'll see how you are tomorrow.'

'But,' I said, preparing to launch into my rehearsed speech. 'But it's the gig at KOKO tonight.'

'That's a shame, but I really don't think you should go. Not even with a slight fever. Do you want me to call someone for you?'

'Yes please, Mum. Could you call Max? Tell him I'm really sorry but there's no way I can make it. Tell him that I'm giving his "plus one" ticket to Vix. I hope he doesn't mind.'

'OK,' said Mum. 'Are you sure you don't want to speak to him?'

'No, honestly. Please call him for me. I don't feel up to it.'

'OK, then. Gosh, Rosie, you really must feel ill. I know how much you've been looking forward to that gig.'

'Yes,' I said, mournfully. 'I've been looking forward to it

for weeks. I guess it just wasn't to be.'

What Mum didn't know was that I'd already given Vix the ticket, the night before. Vix needed some persuading at first, but when I explained why I was doing it, she agreed.

'I really can't go,' I said. 'I don't deserve the ticket. I don't deserve Max. I know for a fact now that I'm going to dump him – as soon as I can – and going to the gig and pretending everything is great wouldn't be fair or right. And, to be honest, I don't really want to see him. It will make it harder. But I can't just let him go on his own, not at the last minute. He likes you, so he'll have a good time with you.'

'OK,' said Vix. 'I can't say I don't want to go. But you love Fieldstar far more than I do. It's an exclusive gig. You're going to have a miserable night, knowing you could be there having a great time.'

'I know,' I said. 'I'll find something to do to cheer myself up, don't worry.'

'And what if Max doesn't want to go with me?'

'He will,' I said.

And, of course, he did.

Now I'm waiting for him to come around to see me. I called him earlier and said I was feeling better, but we needed to talk.

Wish me luck, this is going to be horrible.

Chapter 22
Goodbyes . . . and Hellos

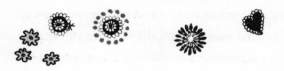

Max is no longer my boyfriend. But I didn't finish with him; in the end he dumped me. Funny how things turn out.

I had a whole speech prepared: how much I liked him, how sweet he was, how much fun I'd had with him, how I wished it could be different . . . but we'd be better off as friends. I didn't get a chance to say any of it. From the moment he arrived at my house, I could tell something had changed. He didn't give me a kiss, not even on the cheek, and he didn't grin as much as usual. He seemed quiet, nervous, lost in his own thoughts. We made small talk about the gig, and how performing with

Fieldstar seemed to have cured Rufus of his depression, and then he came out with it.

'Listen, Rosie,' he said, once he'd made sure that I was feeling better and probably wouldn't die anytime soon. 'I'm just going to say this, before I lose my nerve.' He swallowed, hard. That's when I knew he had his own speech prepared. 'Look,' he continued, 'I don't know about you, but I don't think this is working. Something doesn't feel right. It hasn't for a while. I'm sorry, Rosie, but I'm going back to school soon and I'll be miles away, and I'm not sure what we've got will last the distance.'

Speech over, he sighed and looked at me, expectantly.

All I could manage was, 'Oh.' To tell the truth, I was stunned and – this is weird – sad. I had a lump in my throat and I genuinely felt like I might start crying. Stupid, I know, but realising he didn't want me any more suddenly made me feel like I wanted him. It felt like I'd lost something, even though when I had it, I didn't want it.

'I don't want to hurt you, Rosie,' he said, softly. 'You're a lovely girl. But you deserve more.'

'I know,' I said. 'You too.'

'Friends?'

'Always.'

'I'll come and see you when I visit Rufus, I promise. And we can email if you like.'

'That would be nice.'

'So,' he said. 'I guess this is goodbye, then. I'm going to go back home for a few days, before school starts, to sort stuff out.'

'OK.' I wasn't sure what else to say, or what to do.

'Bye, Rosie.' He leaned over and, putting his arms gently around my back, gave me one final kiss. For the first and the last time with Max, my stomach did a little somersault. And I didn't think about Adam Grigson at all.

So, Max has gone. And Rufus is going away too, tomorrow. Fieldstar are off on a six-month world tour to promote their new album. There's a van outside the house right now, being loaded with Rufus's stuff. Isabella is going on the road with him this time, so the house will be empty. There won't be a celebrity living next door, at least for a while.

Sky is back. She feels terrible about what happened, although nobody really cares about it any more. It turns out that she accidentally told a friend from school who'd emailed her, and that friend told someone else, who told their sister, who knew someone who works at *Sizzling*. She says the reason she didn't reply to my email was because her mum fell out with the yogi at the retreat over 'idealogical differences', whatever that means. Instead of coming home, Sky's mum made the family go on a trek around the island. She got to ride on an elephant and sleep under the stars on the beach. The downside was she didn't have internet access.

I'm with Sky and Vix now, sitting on the roof terrace of a café on Parkway called Tupelo Honey, where you can have home-made cakes and smoothies. We're talking about how rubbish it is that we have to go back to school next week, and how the summer holidays are always far too short. Sky has had her nose pierced. She and her mum both had it done in Goa, and now there's a little red jewel on the side of her right nostril. I think it looks cool (although she'll have to take it out for school), but Sky says she regrets it. She thinks it draws attention to her big nose. Sky doesn't have a big nose. I think she's feeling insecure because she's having problems with Rich again, even though she hoped that a month away would sort everything out. She keeps saying she's not sure how much he missed her. Vix thinks Rich is bad news. She'd never say that to Sky, though.

It's almost seven o'clock now, and I've promised my parents I'll be home for dinner tonight. Linking arms, we leave the café and head back down Parkway, past the cinema, where I saw the weird Japanese romance with Max, and across Britannia Junction. As always, Camden is buzzing. There's a crowd of people standing around outside the tube station, waiting for friends or busking. I can hear the chatter of several different languages and the strains of live music coming from a pub somewhere on the high street. A bearded man wanders around holding a megaphone and shouting that only Jesus

Christ can save us. No one takes any notice of him.

We've just turned into Camden Road and are walking past the bus stop outside Sainsbury's when I hear someone, a guy, shout my name. I can't place the voice.

'Rosie?'

Dropping my friends' arms, I stop and turn around. The bus stop is jammed with people and it takes me a moment to see him. When I do, I can't stop myself from smiling. 'Laurie? Hi.'

He's just as gorgeous as I remember and my stomach is suddenly filled with swooping butterflies. I'm aware that Sky and Vix are up ahead, waiting for me, looking intrigued. I gesture to them to go home and make a telephone shape with my hand.

'Hey, I thought it was you,' says Laurie, coming over to me. He steers me away from the queue. 'Great to bump into you again. How are you?'

'I'm good, thanks. You? Where are you off to?'

'I'm just going to visit a friend. Up in Holloway. Where are you going?'

'Just home,' I say. 'Nothing special.'

'Not going to see the boyfriend tonight, then?'

I feel my face flush. 'Actually, there is no boyfriend. Not any more.'

His eyes twinkle. 'Oh right, that's good. I mean, sorry to hear that.'

'Don't be,' I say. 'It wasn't meant to be. I'm fine about it.'

'Well,' he says, peering at me through his floppy fringe. 'In that case, how about giving me your number?'

Acknowledgements

Thank you to Brenda Gardner, Anne Clark, Elaine McQuade, Melissa Hyder, Natasha Barnden, Simon Davis, Sue Hellard and everyone at Piccadilly Press. Thanks to Stephanie Thwaites and Catherine Saunders at Curtis Brown. Love and unending gratitude to all my family and friends for your support — notably Steve Somerset, Claire Fry, Bibi Lynch, Anthony McGowan, Judy Corre, Anna Corre, Anna Smith, Rachel Baird, Janet Smith and Luisa Plaja of *Chicklish*. Thanks to everyone at the Citea Nice Magnan, especially Marlene, Julie and Mickael. One of these days, you'll be able to read one of my books!

And finally (well, it would be rude not to), thank you to Camden Town, the inspiration for this series, where I have lived happily for seventeen years. If you didn't exist, I'd have to invent you.

CamdenTownTales.co.uk

Get online for:

- Exciting competitions

- The latest on the Camden Town Tales

- Exclusive interview with author Hilary Freeman

- The Insider's Guide to Camden Town

and much more!

Coming Soon

Camden Town Tales

Stuck On Me

Hilary Freeman

When Sky starts fixating on the size of her nose, Rosie and Vix realise they've got their work cut out to boost her self-confidence and stop her doing anything drastic. Little do they know that Sky's obsession will take them on a life-changing journey through parts of Camden Town they've never seen before.